THE CUBE

D0537497

The Cube

Paul Manship

PONT

To my supportive, loving and
much loved wife, Derryn.

Published in 2006 by Pont Books, an imprint of
Gomer Press, Llandysul, Ceredigion SA44 4JL

Second impression – 2008

ISBN 978 1 84323 739 6

A CIP record for this title is available from the British Library.

© Paul Manship, 2006

This book is published with the financial support of the
Welsh Books Council.

Printed and bound in Wales at
Gomer Press, Llandysul, Ceredigion SA44 4JL

Chapter 1

The Cube

One moment it wasn't there.

The next moment it was.

It just sort of . . . popped into being.

Out in Space.

Just beyond Pluto.

A perfect cube.

■　■　■

The first human to spot it was Jim Little, an astronomer working the night-shift in a small observatory in the Australian outback. He was scanning the area just beyond Pluto, hoping to spot the so-called tenth planet (or should it be the ninth, since the International Astronomical Union had decided to reclassify Pluto as a dwarf planet?) when his eyes lighted on something that shouldn't have been there!

Now, when most of your working hours are spent observing spheres, and expecting to see spheres, it's a bit of a shock to find yourself coming face-to-face with a cube! A cube of all things! And a multi-coloured one at that!

At first, Jim assumed that one of his colleagues was larking about with his telescope or the computer.

'Very funny, Sid!' he exclaimed, lurching forward in his chair. 'Nice one, mate!'

But Sid and his other colleagues were not, as Jim suspected, lurking behind a control-panel, having a good giggle at his expense. They were completely oblivious to Jim's discovery, taking a break and discussing the ins and outs of last night's footie.

After checking all his systems, Jim could find no evidence of 'sabotage'. 'Crikey,' he exclaimed, sitting back in his observation chair, 'this can't be happening! No way is that thing real!'

He stared and stared at the object in all its cubic glory! He couldn't take his eyes off it. He scratched his head.

What the heck was it? It was certainly the last thing he'd expected to see when he'd clocked in a few hours earlier. He couldn't have been more taken aback if he'd seen a pink kangaroo floating out there!

He put his eye to the telescope and examined the object more closely.

It looked remarkably like a Rubik's cube. Jim could see nine squares marked out on the cube's most visible face. And there were colours, some of which Jim wasn't quite sure he'd ever seen before.

Of course, there was one major difference between this object and a Rubik's cube. Size! This was a large object. Very large, according to the computer! Jim sunk back into his chair.

Wasn't this the very reason that he'd become an astronomer in the first place? To make new discoveries?

Something brand spanking new had just arrived in the Universe! And who had discovered it? Jim Little. That's who!

A satisfied smile streaked, like a comet, over Jim's face. This object, this thing, this cube, that he had been the first to set eyes on, would forever bear his name.

'The LITTLE Cube!' he announced to himself, enjoying the irony of the object's new name. 'I like the sound of that!' If he could have patted himself on the back, he would have done so.

He picked up the phone. The Australian Government would need to be informed.

■　■　■

Unfortunately, as Jim was soon to discover, he was not the first to have noticed it. For the very nanosecond that the Cube made its entrance into our Universe, a computer in China registered and recorded its existence as Object PK3468.

Of course, for everyday purposes, people would be calling it the Cube.

However, it wouldn't be too long before some of these people would be referring to it as *that* Cube!

And within a few days, many of these people would be wishing that it would go back to wherever it came from.

Chapter 2

Announcement

At the very moment that Jim Little was congratulating himself on his new and important discovery, eleven-year-old Tyrone Davies stood shivering in the goalmouth of his school's football pitch, on the other side of the world.

South Wales, to be specific.

Rhiwderin Junior School.

Rhiwderin at home to Pentrepoeth.

Tyrone was wearing a bright yellow goalkeeper's jersey and dreaming about the roast lamb that his mum would be cooking him for tea.

He knew why he'd been put in goals. And it wasn't because of his athletic ability. It was because he was the largest boy in Year Six.

Large, as in tall, and large, as in, well . . .

His nan liked to refer to him as 'cuddly', which was a polite way of putting it. Some of Tyrone's team-mates had other, less polite, ways of putting it.

They were losing 5–0 and the rest of the team had made it clear whose fault they thought it was. Tyrone had only volunteered to go in goals because nobody else wanted to. What a mistake!

He'd never realized before how violent football could be! He understood that he was supposed to get the ball off his opponents – but there were lots of them and only one of him. Rugby players could expect to dive onto a frost-hardened pitch. But footballers? And so, Tyrone had stood by and watched as the opposing team booted the ball past him five times.

In any case, where were the Rhiwderin defenders? For all Tyrone knew, they could have emigrated!

Uh-oh! Pentrepoeth's Number Nine was on the attack again, swerving towards him, this way and that, like a human snake.

'Come out, Davies!!!' Tyrone heard Mr Munkley, his head teacher, bellow from the sidelines.

Tyrone took in a deep breath, plucked up every ounce of courage and started edging towards the attacker, spreading his arms wide, trying to cover all the angles. The Rhiwderin defenders were completely out of position, so Tyrone was on his own. He made a sudden dive, just as the attacker decided to chip the ball over him. Tyrone rolled over in time to watch it float, as if in slow motion, into the back of his net.

The final whistle went.

Tyrone sat up and watched as his team-mates walked off the pitch, their heads bowed low. He heard Mr Munkley mutter, 'My granny could play better than that!'

There were pats on backs all round as dads commiserated with their sons. 'Never mind, butty! Better luck next time!'

Rhodri Lloyd's dad caught Tyrone's eye, winked at him and shouted across, jovially, 'All right Cinderella? Missed the ball again, did you?' How hilarious!

Goalkeepers were supposed to save the day, not ruin it for everybody! Tyrone closed his eyes and prayed for a huge hole to appear in the goal-mouth and swallow him up. But it didn't.

And just to top it all, when he arrived home half an hour later, he discovered that there was no roast lamb waiting for him. Not even cheese-on-toast!

He found his mum sitting in front of the telly, seemingly transfixed, along with his dad, his teenage brother, Terry, his nan, who lived with them, and their next-door-neighbour, Mrs Phillips, who didn't but thought she did.

For one minute, Tyrone thought his whole family had been hypnotized by the television. They were all staring at it, open-mouthed. Even his nan's budgie seemed to be in a trance.

Then Terry noticed his younger brother. 'Hey, bro, come and look at this!'

As all the other seats were occupied, Tyrone sat himself down on the floor. He stared at the strange multi-coloured object that filled the TV screen. 'What is it?' he asked.

'Nobody knows,' said his dad.

'It's a mystery,' said Nan.

'Ooooh,' squawked the budgie.

The Cube, Tyrone was soon to learn, had been sitting there in Outer Space, inviting questions, interpretations and explanations for the last six hours.

But then, a few minutes after Tyrone had plonked himself down on the carpet, it suddenly disappeared from the TV screen, to be replaced by a panel of 'experts' on a special edition of *Wales Today*. These, it soon transpired, had no answers whatsoever to the questions that everyone was asking.

What is it? Who made it? How did it get here? What does it want?

The Welsh astronomer Ifor Wynford-Thomas declared self-importantly, 'To me, this object implies the existence of dimensions other than our own. I would suggest that it is an alien life-form which has arrived through a worm-hole and possesses a vastly superior intelligence to our own . . .'

Archbishop Vaughan Willams cleared his throat, interrupting, 'There is only one greater intelligence than ours. Following the logic of your argument, then this Cube must, in fact, be God.'

'That is a strong probability,' concurred the mathematician from the University of Wales. 'From a mathematical standpoint, if I were God, a cube would be a good choice. After all, it's perfect. A sphere would have been good too but I suppose there are enough of those up there already . . .'

Aliens? God? Tyrone was completely bewildered. He was expecting to come home to roast lamb and *The Simpsons*, not God and aliens!

Suddenly there was a flurry as the panel members were interrupted by an urgent newsflash.

The Cube had decided to communicate.

The Davies family sat in silence as the Cube seemed to vibrate and a gentle, soothing female voice emanated from it:

GREETINGS AND SALUTATIONS!

IT HAS COME TO OUR ATTENTION THAT THERE HAS BEEN TOO MUCH ARGUING LATELY IN THIS SECTOR OF THE UNIVERSE.

IN ORDER TO HELP RESOLVE MATTERS, WE WOULD LIKE TO MAKE A PROPOSAL:

ONE MAJOR LIFE FORM WILL BE CHOSEN, AT RANDOM, FROM EACH OF THE SEVEN LIFE-BEARING PLANETS IN YOUR SOLAR SYSTEM.

THESE WILL BE TRANSPORTED TO THE CUBE, WHERE THEY WILL TAKE PART IN A GAME.

FURTHER DETAILS WILL FOLLOW . . .

Stunned silence in the Davies household. Even the budgie was lost for words!

Tyrone was confused. Firstly, what the heck was going on? Secondly, how come the message was in English? What about his cousin Maldwyn in Aber? Did he hear it in Welsh? And thirdly, what about people of other nationalities? People in France, for example, or Norway or Outer Mongolia?

Watching the news a few hours later, he discovered that all nations on Earth had received the message in their own language. Strange or what?

The reaction of most people to the Cube's announcement was: 'A game? Is that it?!' It no longer seemed mysterious and exciting. It had now become something ridiculous, something to laugh at.

Tyrone's mum noticed that the message had said *We will choose . . .*

'That means there's more than one of them,' she nodded. Her husband frowned at her.

'One major life form from each of the life-bearing planets,' Terry mused at Tweety-Pie in her cage just above his dad's head. 'I wonder if budgies count?'

'They're not taking my Tweety!' Nan called out.

Tyrone went upstairs for a bath, praying that he wasn't the major life form chosen from this planet. He'd gone right off any sort of competitive games!

Chapter 3

Standstill

The Cube was the major focus of attention in Rhiwderin Junior School the next day.

Everybody was talking about it – the children, the teachers, the secretary, the caretaker, the dinner supervisors, the canteen staff, the cleaners.

Some anxious parents decided to keep their children at home. After all, who could say with confidence what the Cube's intentions were?

Tyrone had tried his best to persuade his dad to let him stay at home, especially after yesterday's disastrous goalkeeping performance, but he didn't get the response he wanted. 'No way, Sunny Jim. I don't know about other families but the Davies household is going to carry on as normal. There's not a lot we can do about some object floating out in space, 7,500 million kilometres away, is there?'

Tyrone's dad was quite right – and remarkably accurate too! The Cube *was* 7,500 million kilometres away, give or take a few thousand kilometres.

And there was absolutely nothing anyone in Wales or anywhere else on the planet could do about it!

The main topic of conversation on the schoolyard at ten to nine was predictable: who was going to be chosen as the major life form from Earth?

'It's gonna be Ryan Poyner, I just know it is,' declared Megan Hall, with complete confidence.

'Why?'

''Cos he's just lush, he is!'

Tyrone wandered around on his own, trying without much success, to avoid thinking about it. The chances of him being chosen had to be a few billion-to-one. Besides, they'd probably choose an adult.

Nobody mentioned yesterday's football match, thank goodness. The Cube had saved him from that, at least!

Even in the classroom, Tyrone couldn't get away from it. The timetable went out of the window and a special agenda of Cube-related activities was arranged.

For maths, he and his classmates practised finding surface areas and volumes of various boxes, and then they constructed cubes and cuboids, using straws.

And, after maths, Mr Morgan decided to combine history and RE and have a discussion about relationships with our interplanetary neighbours.

'Of course,' he said, sitting on Carwyn Clements's desk and squashing his Cardiff City pencil case, 'we only found out we had neighbours five years ago. Does anybody remember how?'

Joshua Maybry raised his arm. 'Well, sir, World War Three was about to kick off, because of some disagreement over oil. The President had his finger poised over the red button, ready to give the order to deploy nuclear weapons, when our "neighbours" started to reveal themselves.'

Joshua Maybry knew a lot of stuff about a lot of

stuff. Now, *he'd* be an ideal candidate to take part in the Game, thought Tyrone.

'Well put, Josh,' said Mr Morgan. 'Now, who remembers which of our neighbours was the first to communicate with us?'

Who could *not* remember? They'd seen it replayed on TV often enough. Nobody was likely to forget the moment when the first Martian appeared on terrestrial TV screens. Some people immediately assumed it was a devil. The red scaly skin, horns on the head and claw-like hands may have had something to do with it.

But it wasn't a devil. In fact, the Martian turned out to be quite a cool and level-headed fellow. His message to the people of Earth ran something like this, 'Hey, Earth-dudes, for your sake and the sake of the rest of the Solar System, you people need to chill out.'

Mr Morgan stood up and started to wander around. Carwyn Clements retrieved his squashed pencil case, dangling it in front of him like an expiring fish.

'And what effect did this message have on the President and other world leaders?'

Not a lot, Tyrone seemed to remember!

It was the cumulative effect of messages from the other planetary neighbours that finally did the trick.

A few hours after the Martian broadcast, with the President still pondering whether or not to press the button, a Neptunian rocket swooped past the presidential palace, trailing the following message in a swirl of blue cloud:

GIVE PEACE A CHANCE

This certainly gave pause for thought, but the killer punch had come from Jupiter. Using the latest technology, they succeeded in sending the following email to every computer on our planet:

If you persist with these reckless intentions, then you will be sorry, VERY SORRY.

Now this had the desired effect!

Nobody knew a lot about Jupiter, except that it was approximately 1,300 times bigger than Earth! Perhaps the politicians and generals considered the possibility that Jupiter's nuclear weapons might also be 1,300 times bigger!

And so it was, Tyrone remembered his dad telling him, that in a remarkably short period of time – a few minutes actually – the warring nations of Earth put their petty differences aside and became the best of buddies. One huge brotherhood of man (and woman).

Mr Morgan continued. 'Can anyone tell us how long this period of peace lasted?'

It hadn't been long, Tyrone remembered.

'Six days,' declared Joshua Maybry confidently.

Was there anything Joshua Maybry didn't know?

'Correctamundo, Josh – the Six Day Peace.' Mr Morgan now stood at the front of the class, his elbow resting on top of his whiteboard. 'Well, that's enough historical background. Has anybody got any bright ideas about this Cube?'

'It's a hoax, sir,' shouted out Simon Fisher. 'Just like the Apollo moon landings. It's fake. There isn't really a cube out there. It's just some kind of special effect.' He sat back in his chair, arms folded, with a satisfied look on his face.

Tyrone had seen a programme on the history channel which set out to show that men hadn't really landed on the Moon. It was quite convincing.

Nicola Graham put her hand up. 'I think it's a sign from God, sir. To make us stop arguing and fighting.'

Mr Morgan nodded his head vigorously. 'I like that idea, Nicola. As the Cube said in its message, there has been an awful lot of arguing in our Solar System over the last five years. Can anyone name any examples?'

Who couldn't? There were so many to choose from.

Perhaps, after all, it had been a good thing that our neighbouring planets had kept such a low profile for so long because, within six days of becoming acquainted with each other, we managed to find one thousand and one things to argue about.

Within a very short time span, Planet Earth had become involved in a squabble with Saturn. Soon after that, we'd became majorly miffed with both Mercury and Mars. And then there developed a serious vendetta with Venus. The only planets with which we managed to avoid any trouble were Uranus and Pluto (because, it turned out, they didn't have any inhabitants) and Jupiter (because, frankly, they scared the pants off us)!

Many of the arguments didn't even involve us! The other planets managed to find plenty to fight about on their own. There were constant rows and rivalries, scrapes and scuffles, feuds, duels and quarrels!

And what were the fights about?

Anything and everything! You name it, it led to a fight!

'I can think of one, sir,' said Alex Leighton. 'There was that time when a Martian flying saucer accidentally crash-landed into one of Venus's most important monuments.'

'Yes, good one,' said Mr Morgan, 'and do you remember what the Venusians did in response?'

Alex paused. 'They built a flying cup (to match the flying saucer) and sent it crashing into the peak of Mount Olympus, the highest, or ex-highest mountain on Mars. Quite clever, really.'

'Well, it certainly caused a stir,' said Mr Morgan, laughing at his own joke. 'Does anyone remember any other incidents?'

'Yes, sir,' said Joshua I-know-everything Maybry. 'There's the ongoing problem with Mercury.'

'Which is?'

'They've been accused by the other planets of absorbing an unfair amount of the Sun's energy.'

Mr Morgan nodded. 'And what do the Mercurians say in their defence?'

'They say, sir, it's hardly their fault that their planet is nearer to the Sun than all the others. And, furthermore, would the other planets like to swap places and try living next to an enormous ball of flame and gas?'

Mr Morgan then pointed out that our own planet was not complaint-free. We'd been accused by more than one of our neighbours of overcrowding airspace with our satellites, shuttles and space-stations; of dumping chemical-and-nuclear-waste; and of showing no respect for the plants and animals that share our eco-system.

Mr Morgan sat back down on Carwyn's desk, squashing his pencil case for the second time. 'In my opinion,' he declared, 'this Cube has arrived in the nick of time! Hopefully, it will help stop all this interplanetary bickering before it develops into something more serious.'

Since the Cube's arrival twenty hours ago, all bickering had ceased. All disputes had come to a standstill. There was now something else to focus on!

'On the other hand, sir,' pondered Simon Fisher, 'perhaps it's come to blow us all away!'

The classroom became quiet. Simon Fisher had struck a chord. Nobody really knew what the Cube's true intentions were.

It could be a force for good.

Or it could be something else.

Something that didn't bear thinking about . .

Chapter 4

The Game

Nothing happened for a week.

The Cube made no further announcements. It just sat there, in Space, and on people's television screens, generating questions and theories.

Waiting.

But, exactly seven days later, Tyrone was on his way through the front door, heading for school, when his nan called him back.

'Ty! Ty!' she called out. 'It's speaking again!'

At first he thought she meant the budgie. Nan was the only one who heard Tweety-pie speak and was convinced the bird was trying to deliver some message from her husband, who'd died before Tyrone was born. But it wasn't Tweety-pie. It was the Cube.

Tyrone stood in the living-room doorway and listened to the new message:

THE CHOSEN LIFE FORMS WILL BE
TRANSPORTED TO THE CUBE, WHERE THEY
WILL PARTICIPATE IN A GAME.

EACH CONTESTANT WILL ACT AS A
REPRESENTATIVE FOR HIS, HER OR ITS PLANET.

AT THE END OF THE GAME THERE WILL BE ONE
WINNER AND, NEEDLESS TO SAY, SIX LOSERS.

There was quite a long pause:

THE LOSERS WILL FIND THEMSELVES WITHOUT
PLANETS TO GO HOME TO.

Another pause. Tyrone joined his nan on the sofa.
She and the budgie were doing goldfish impressions.
Then:

WE SINCERELY HOPE THAT THE WINNING
PLANET WILL LEARN TO LIVE IN
HARMONY WITH ITSELF.

Silence enveloped the living-room at Number 22.

It also enveloped the rest of Tredegar Street, the rest
of Rhiwderin, the rest of Wales, the rest of the planet
and the rest of the Solar System.

A great, cavernous ssshhhhh that stretched itself all
the way from Mercury to Pluto.

'Blinking 'eck!' Tyrone's nan exclaimed, dropping her
knitting. She held her grandson's hand.

Suddenly, everything had become deadly serious. This
was no longer an exciting puzzle or just a bit of
fun. Tyrone thought back to what Simon Fisher had
said: perhaps it had come to blow us all away.

Not funny anymore.

■ ■ ■

23

On a global level, the silence soon transformed itself into anger. One irate general proclaimed, 'We don't have to take this from some uppity 3-D shape. Somebody fetch me some nukes!'

But it was almost as if the Cube was psychic; it made a further brief announcement a few hours later:

YOU WILL FIND THAT ANY THREATENING ACTION USED AGAINST THE CUBE WILL RESULT IN DIRE CONSEQUENCES FOR THE PERPETRATOR.

ANY MISSILES SENT IN THIS DIRECTION WILL BE REPELLED AND RETURNED TO THEIR POINT OF ORIGIN, FULLY-ARMED.

Oh.

Chapter 5

The Chosen One

Tyrone sat with his nan for a few minutes, just to make sure she wasn't going to have a stroke or a heart attack or something, then left for school.

He bumped into Joshua Maybry right outside his front door. Mr Know-It-All was bubbling with excitement. 'Hey, have you heard?' he said.

'Of course I've heard,' said Tyrone, still in a state of shock. 'I do live on this planet, y'know.'

As they continued on their way to school, Joshua bounded up and down. 'I hope I get picked for this game thing,' he exclaimed. 'I'd show those other planets a thing or two . . .'

I bet you would, thought Tyrone.

'. . . I'd be the most famous person that ever lived!'

Tyrone frowned. 'And what if you didn't win? Have you thought of that?'

Joshua stopped bouncing for a moment. He declared, 'I don't see how I could possibly lose, do you? Everyone knows I'm the cleverest person in the school.'

'Have you stopped to think,' said Tyrone, as they came to the bottom of Tredegar Street, 'that, even if you did win, you'd be responsible for the destruction of six other planets.'

Josh shrugged and headed into the corner shop. 'Yeh,

but that wouldn't be my fault. I didn't invent the game, did I? You can blame the Cube for that!'

Tyrone shook his head in disbelief. 'Anyway,' he said, changing the subject, 'I've got more immediate things to worry about. We're playing Glasllwch after school today and I'm in goals again.'

Josh sniggered. 'You don't mean to say they picked you after last week's performance?'

Tyrone frowned. 'They haven't got anybody else, have they!'

■ ■ ■

Four o' clock found Tyrone in the same position he'd been in exactly a week ago when the Cube had first been spotted by Jim Little. He was making a much better effort this time and had only let two goals slip by him so far, but he was still soaking up a lot of abuse from the sidelines and from players on both teams!

It was turning colder. Tea-time soon! Bangers and mash!

The opposition goalkeeper had possession of the ball and gave it a massive boot up the pitch. It landed right in front of a line of three Glasllwch forwards. One of them got control of the ball and off they headed towards Tyrone, like a three-headed, six-footed monster. *Here we go again*, thought Tyrone. *Not a defender in sight!*

'Come on Cinders!' Rhodri Lloyd's dad shouted encouragingly. 'You *shall* go to the ball!'

Tyrone's legs were moving but he wasn't going

26

anywhere yet. He had to judge it just right. He'd make his move on the next touch.

The boy with the ball took one look at Tyrone, smirked and called out to his fellow forwards, 'Here comes my hat trick, lads! There's no way Blubber-boy's gonna get this!'

Tyrone burst into action. He was going to get that ball, and if, by chance, he wasn't quick enough, he was going to take great pleasure in knocking the wind out of his loud-mouthed opponent!

Like a charging bull, he drove forward, head down. He had one eye on the ball and the other on Big-mouth's muddy kneecaps.

Decisions, decisions. The ball or the kneecaps? He dived and closed his eyes at the same time, ready for impact . . .

Only there was no impact.

Nothing.

Tyrone opened his eyes.

He didn't have a clue what had just happened. The three attackers were no longer there. They'd vanished.

Along with the rest of the team.

And the sports field!

And the school!

And everything else!

Maybe I've been knocked unconscious, Tyrone thought. He wasn't feeling any pain, but he did feel slightly dizzy and he could see sparkly white dots floating all around him.

And someone had switched off all the sound!

Chapter 6

Tek

The only things Tyrone could see were his own body, lots of sparkly white dots and lots and lots of blackness.

He was still on his hands and knees, but there didn't appear to be anything substantial underneath them!

He turned to his right – blackness, white dots.

He turned to his left – more of the same.

He struggled to his feet and swivelled round to look behind him. Aaaaaaaarrrrrrgggghhhhh!!!!!

He found himself face-to-face with a monstrous head! He would have fallen backwards in horror if there'd been anything to fall on!

What was this thing doing on Rhiwderin Junior School football pitch? Come to think of it, where was the football pitch!?

Tyrone had seen scary, ugly things before – Martian beauty contests on interplanetary TV, his brother's girlfriend without any make-up – but nothing compared to the face that was hovering in front of his nose right this minute. It was just hideous! A bulldog chewing a wasp would have to be prettier!

The head was attached to a body some distance away from it by an enormously long and snake-like neck. The body was about seven feet tall. The head remained eye-to-eye with Tyrone, examining him intently.

As Tyrone backed away, he could see that the creature was wearing a long crimson-coloured coat with gold stitching and buttons. The outfit and the face didn't go together at all! The overall effect was that of a doorman to some swish intergalactic hotel.

If Tyrone's vocal cords had been working, no doubt he would have blurted out *W-w-who are you?* or *W-w-where am I?* or *W-w-what do you want?*

The creature blinked and spoke. The movements its lips were making did not coincide at all with the words that Tyrone could hear. It was like watching a dubbed foreign movie.

'Please do not be alarmed, young sir,' it said, in a gentle, reassuring voice. 'It is my responsibility and, may I say, pleasure, to welcome you here.'

Pleasure? thought Tyrone. 'Buh, buh . . . buh, buh, buh . . .' he said.

Any moment now, he thought, *I'll come round. The ball will be in the back of the net and it will be 3–0 to Glasllwch. Everything will be all right.*

But he did not come round and everything was not all right!

In fact, things took a turn for the worse.

To his horror and alarm, a menagerie of strange creatures started popping into existence all around him. They just appeared, out of thin air, much as the Cube had done. There were six 'pops' altogether.

Tyrone spun around slowly, hemmed in on all sides by odd-looking beings, one half his size, two twice his size, one black, one red and one green!

Then they all started to speak at the same time. After

29

listening to their various squawks, squeals, shouts, screams, screeches and sobs, Tyrone knew that these creatures were not a threat or danger at all but were, in fact, in pretty much the same predicament as he was.

And then it struck him! Like a sledgehammer!

Including himself, there were seven creatures assembled here! Seven creatures. Seven life forms from seven planets. Surely not.

Six and a half billion people living on Planet Earth and who gets chosen? Tyrone Davies from Rhiwderin, South Wales! That's who! How was this possible?

Week in, week out, his dad did the lottery – and never won a penny! And yet a mysterious cube appears in Space and chooses him out of six and a half billion people!

Tyrone wanted out, right then and there! He definitely wasn't up to this challenge, this responsibility! He couldn't think of anybody less suited to competitive games than him. Why couldn't they have chosen some athlete instead? Like Joe Calzaghe or Gavin Henson!

His doubts and misgivings were interrupted by the creature with the crimson coat and bulldog features. 'My dear creatures, please remain calm. All will be explained. Let me introduce myself. I am known as the Technician. But you may call me Tek. I have no doubt that you are all a little bewildered and perhaps even frightened. Well, I am the bearer of good news. You have been selected, as representatives of your home-planets, to participate in a, in a . . .'

'Game?' offered Tyrone.

'Exactly. Thank you, young sir. The game will take place inside the Cube.'

More squawks and squeals.

Tek retracted his head, like a tortoise, back into his body and then reached down to his chest and fiddled with something hanging around his neck. 'Ahem. From this point on, for the purposes of the game, each of you will be able to communicate with your fellow contestants and any other creatures with whom you come into contact.'

There was a pause, giving the contestants time to reflect on why they had been chosen. Some seemed pleased, others not so.

Then Tyrone heard himself say out loud, 'Where is the Cube?'

'Yeah,' added the red-skinned creature next to him, presumably the representative from Mars, 'have you lost it or something?'

Tek looked amused and shook his head. 'If you would all care to raise your heads ninety degrees, I think you will find what you are looking for.'

As one, seven heads looked up.

Tyrone felt instantly off-balance. It's not a pleasant feeling to find a huge object hovering above your head!

The Cube was a lot larger than Tyrone had imagined it to be. On the telly, it had seemed miniscule; up close, it was bigger than Caerphilly Castle. Only not so interesting to look at. No arrow-holes, no turrets or towers, no battlements, no door. Just a cube, really.

But a very BIG one!

If there's no door, thought Tyrone, *then how are we supposed to get in? Unless, the door's around the other side.*

In fact, the door could be on any one of six faces.

It could be on the top!

As if reading Tyrone's thoughts, Tek declared, 'You may be wondering, my dear creatures, how anybody gets inside the Cube.'

Many nodding heads.

'Well,' Tek continued, raising his upper limbs in the air, 'wonder no longer!' And then, as an afterthought, 'Please stand to one side!'

What happened next took them all by surprise!

The Cube was constructed exactly like a Rubik's cube: twenty-six outer cubes surrounding an inner cube. Without warning, the outer cubes separated themselves from the central block, one of them narrowly missing the contestants.

'Woh!' Tyrone heard himself say.

'Woh is right!!' commented the Martian, whose name was Rufus Blade.

Tyrone looked to his left, to his right, in front, behind and below. He could still just about see the cubes, but they had travelled a very long distance in a very short space of time!

Impressive, thought Tyrone. *Now what?*

The remaining cube glowed into life. It started to hum and vibrate, then slowly descended towards them.

There was nowhere to run.

'Don't like it,' commented a rather babyish voice from deep in the huddle as the glowing white cube lowered itself over and through the contestants.

Once they were all safely inside, the outer cubes shot

back into position, each one connecting with a resounding clunk!

They were all now well and truly inside the Cube.

The blackness of Space was gone. They were now enveloped in dazzling, almost blinding whiteness. Tyrone couldn't see the other cubes. All he could see was the whiteness surrounding the other contestants. He had to half-close his eyes to block out the glare.

Surrounded by so much white, Tyrone felt insignificant – even more insignificant than usual.

Just as he was adjusting his eyesight to this new environment, it changed yet again. Tyrone became aware of a buzz and a flicker, as if someone were switching channels, and then the whiteness was gone!

What replaced it was what looked like the Great Hall of a medieval castle, complete with huge wooden banqueting table, multi-coloured shields and flaming torches mounted on the walls.

These rapid changes were very unnerving and Tyrone stayed as close to the others as possible.

Tek remained still and calm. 'My dear creatures . . .' he declared.

'If he says that just one more time,' muttered Rufus Blade, 'I'm gonna tie a knot in that neck of his!'

'My dear creatures,' Tek reiterated, frowning at Rufus, 'I shall shortly be leaving you, so that you can become better acquainted with each other. If you would care to sit down, food will be arriving shortly. Then, after you have rested, the game will commence.'

With that, he melted into the air and was gone.

Chapter 7

The Seven

Seven chairs were arranged around the table but there was only one that looked of any consequence.

The second that Tek vanished, there was a frantic scuffle as three members of the group started pushing and pulling each other in an effort to occupy the throne-like chair positioned at the head of the table.

It didn't take long for the matter to be resolved, for JW Ganymede, a huge cat-like creature from Jupiter, grabbed his two challengers by the scruff of the neck, flung them to one side as if they were rag dolls and then proceeded to wriggle and squeeze his enormously proportioned behind into the 'throne'.

Once he was snugly settled, a grin wider than the Milky Way spread across his face. He waved his paw grandly and exclaimed, 'Why don't y'all make yourselves comfortable!'

To Tyrone, he sounded like an American oil-tycoon. The Cube's choice of voice-translator showed it had a sense of humour.

JW Ganymede was by far the largest creature in the group, about twice as tall as Tyrone and three times as wide. Although vaguely cat-like in appearance, he was fur-less (more rubbery than furry) and his ears were droopy like a spaniel's. His body resembled a huge balloon, stained with horizontal bands, some light, some dark, some wide, some narrow.

The Martian, Rufus Blade – one of the two unfortunates now sitting on the floor – looked very disgruntled. 'Hey,' he gestured, 'why don't you make yourself at home, fat boy? Who do you think you are? I can't wait to see what happens when I stick a pin in you, you big bag of wind!'

Rufus looked ready to do battle. All fired up and clad in black leather and metal studs, he looked like a biker-warrior, nothing like the chilled-out Martians they'd seen on TV.

Tyrone would soon discover that, far from being calm, the Martian temperament was extremely changeable and could alternate quite unexpectedly between total chill-out and exploding volcano.

By the look on his face, it was clear that JW Ganymede wasn't used to being spoken to like this. He slammed his hefty paw down onto the table.

'How dare you address me in that manner!' he protested. 'Why, back on my home planet, I'll have you know, I could have you incarcerated for speaking to me in that fashion!'

Rufus got to his feet and found himself a chair. 'Well, dude, in case you haven't noticed, you ain't back on your planet, so give us all a break! And, by the way, the next time you lay your hands on me, you'd better be ready for some major comeback!'

The two protagonists glared at each other, while the other contestants took their seats.

Fortunately, a new voice intervened. A female voice.

35

'Does anyone know when the grub's comin' 'cos I be blummin' starvin'?'

All heads turned towards the new voice which, to Tyrone's ear, sounded like it belonged in Cornwall, not on another planet.

The creature's name was Daphne Gorge and she was from Venus. Her most prominent features were a pair of wonderfully expressive eyes with enormous eye-lashes, and pouting pink lips. These would have been fine on a model or film-star but looked out-of-place on a short, squat carnivorous plant, which is what she was.

Her 'hair' was swept back in a swathe of tropical greenery. Her arms, if that's what you could call them, consisted of two huge leaves, rolled up compactly and glistening with condensation. Folds of flabby green flesh undulated beneath her many chins.

She continued, 'I 'aven't eaten fr'about two hours. I'll be wastin' away afore long, I will!'

There's not much danger of that, looking at the size of you, thought Tyrone. But he was definitely feeling hungry. His bangers and mash were now a distant memory – no doubt still waiting for him in the kitchen.

As if on cue, the food was brought in.

It was fast food. Very fast food!

There was only one waiter, as far as Tyrone could make out, but what a waiter! He moved so fast, he was blurred at the edges. He made seven journeys to and from the 'kitchen' in less than half a minute. He finished serving before anyone had a chance to say 'Can I have some tomato-sauce?'

The seven contestants stared at the steaming plates before them. Their faces registered pleasant surprise.

'Hey, buddy,' Rufus said, nudging Tyrone's elbow, 'I hate to say it but I think you got the short straw. That looks disgusting. What are those little orange things?'

Tyrone took a deep, satisfied breath and grinned at the prospect of the food in front of him. 'This is egg, beans and chips and I defy anyone in the Universe to find anything more delicious!'

'If you say so. Looks revolting.'

The Cube had been very thoughtful in planning the menu. The atmosphere in the Hall became relaxed and jovial as everyone tucked into his or her favourite food.

At the head of the table, JW Ganymede appeared to be dipping jelly-babies into some hot, bubbling soup. Each one emitted a short, squeaking sound as he bit into it. 'These are, without doubt, theee most deee-lectable mush-mush it has ever been my privilege to eat!' he announced.

'What are – mush-mush?' Tyrone enquired.

JW held one up for all to see. It wriggled. 'Well,' he pondered, 'I suppose they're a little bit like your caterpillars. We like to eat 'em just before they turn into flitterglides.'

Tyrone suddenly felt ill.

To his immediate right, Rufus was digging into something called 'craterballs'. They were grey and lumpy, about two centimetres in diameter. They looked like little boulders.

'Watch this, sunbeam,' Rufus said, nudging Tyrone.

Tyrone watched as Rufus raised a craterball to his

lips, smiled in anticipation, then bit down on it. Immediately his face turned from red to purple and steam was expelled from his nostrils and ears.

He shook his head violently from side to side until the effect wore off. 'Man, that was good!' he declared. 'I like my food hot! And that was hot! Zoweeee!!!'

As the steam cleared, Tyrone became aware of the two huge silver trays sitting in front of Daphne Gorge, loaded with what looked like large chunks of eel.

Rufus nudged Tyrone again. 'Hey, bro, I'd like to see how she's gonna get those huge fishy chunks in her mouth without smudging her lipstick.'

They then both looked on in horror as she reached down with her leafy arms, inserted them into her green, glistening belly, pulled outwards and managed to create a huge hole in it. She then proceeded to shovel in the lumps of rotting eel. The effect was stomach-churning.

In less than a minute, the silver trays were empty.

With all the food gone, Daphne, by some unknown method, folded her belly back together again.

Tyrone switched his attention to the little creature to his left, the one who had been foolish enough to compete with Rufus and JW for the throne.

'What have you got there?' he asked.

The little creature eyed Tyrone suspiciously and wrapped his spiky black arms protectively around his food, a collection of what seemed to be spirals made from pink ice. 'Me got frozzles,' he said defensively.

He was a very strange-looking being. Tyrone remembered seeing a story-book when he was in Rhiwderin Infants with a picture of Jack Frost. The little creature to his left reminded him of that picture, only instead of being frosty-white, he was crispy-black. He was all sharp edges, skeletally thin, and appeared to be made of coal. Wisps of smoke billowed from him. His name was Spindle.

'You sure do have a lot there, boy!' observed JW Ganymede who had just eaten his last mush-mush. 'Far too many for a little feller like you.'

Daphne Gorge chirped in, 'I jes' been countin' 'em an' there's eighteen, if I'm not mistaken.'

JW twiddled with his whiskers. 'How about sharing some around, buddy? I don't know about my friends here, but I could do with a nice refreshing dessert!'

Spindle's reaction was to pull the frozzles closer to him. 'MY FROZZLES!' he reiterated, with venom.

JW tut-tutted. 'I think we get the picture. Y'know, back home on my planet, my daddy would have whipped me for such blatant bad manners.'

'Not your planet,' said Spindle and then, in less than two minutes, polished off all eighteen frozzles, pink liquid dripping from his pointed chin.

This was a real conversation-stopper and the others could only look on in amazement and disgust. The silence was broken by Rufus Blade. His attention had switched to the other end of the table. 'Hey, girlie, you haven't said much!'

In fact, the 'girlie' hadn't spoken at all.

She sat very tall and upright in her silvery robes. Long white hair fell past her shoulders. If it wasn't for the fact that her ears were a little too pointy, her skin a little too pale and her nose a little too turned up, she would have been beautiful.

She put down her knife and fork. 'If I'd heard anything worth responding to, I would have spoken.'

She sounded like someone who'd seen and done everything and found it all just too, too boring.

'What's your name, doll-face?' Rufus asked, to Tyrone's amusement.

'Well it's certainly not doll-face!' she said sternly. 'My name is Grace Peak.'

'Pleased to meet you, doll-face. I'm Rufus Bl . . .'

'I know who you are,' she interrupted. 'I know who you all are.'

'That's impossible, young lady,' declared JW Ganymede.

Grace Peak stood up – all seven foot of her! Her shadow fell right along the table. 'You are JW Ganymede from Jupiter. To your left is Rufus Blade from Mars. To his left is Tyrone Davies from Earth. Opposite me is Spindle from Mercury. To my left is Daphne Gorge from Venus. And to her left is Alpha Minor from Neptune.'

JW sat back in his throne, flabbergasted.

Nobody had noticed the dolphin-like creature, Alpha Minor, who was sitting to Daphne Gorge's left. He was nibbling daintily on some seaweed.

Now finding himself the centre of attention, he paused and spoke.

'I am very happy to make all your acquaintances. Please call me Alph.'

Tyrone found his voice calm and soothing although strangely his mouth didn't seem to move.

Everybody else seemed to have noticed too.

JW joked, 'Are you a ventriloquist or somethin', boy?'

Alpha Minor's eyes smiled and he spoke again. 'Apologies. I should have explained before. On my planet, we communicate telepathically.'

'Telly-what-ically?' said JW.

'We use our minds, rather than our voices,' Alph clarified. 'I believe Miss Grace Peak also has telepathic skills, which may explain how she knows so much about us.'

Grace Peak flicked her hair in exasperation. 'Thank you, but I don't need anybody to do my explaining for me.'

'Hey, cool it, chickie,' Rufus intervened, raising his hand. 'Alphie here was only trying to help. Boy, you've sure got some attitude there, girlie.'

Grace Peak pounded her fist on the table, 'I am NOT your girlie and I am NOT your chickie, or anyone else's, for that matter!'

'That's fine by me. Girlie!'

And then, quite unexpectedly, two beams of light shot from Grace's eyes. Rufus's serviette burst into flames, causing him to fall backwards out of his chair. He struggled to his feet, looking even redder than normal. 'Boy, are you gonna pay for that!'

Without warning, the creature called Tek re-materialized.

Right in the middle of the table.

It looked like somebody had chopped him in half and

41

stuck the top half of his body onto the table. 'My dear creatures, my dear creatures,' he said cheerily, 'I'm so pleased to see that you're getting to know each other.'

Rufus was on his feet and heading towards Grace Peak.

'Please sit down, Master Blade,' Tek urged. 'Perhaps I neglected to explain to you that any contestant who deliberately harms another will be automatically disqualified from the game. And I think you know what that means.'

Rufus scowled and sat back down, giving Grace a glare, which was duly returned.

Tek continued, rotating slowly as he spoke. 'I sincerely hope that you enjoyed your meal. You will now have a brief opportunity to rest. During the game itself you will have no respite. I can assure you that you will need all your physical and mental energy.'

With a buzz and a flicker, the Great Hall was gone. It was replaced by a circular room, a dormitory. Seven beds of various sizes, arranged like the spokes of a wheel. This time, there was no frantic scuffling for the best one. The various sizes and shapes made choosing logical and easy.

Tyrone sat on the end of his bed. He was feeling very edgy. 'How will we know when the game has started?' he said to no-one in particular.

'It probably already has,' muttered Rufus.

'There will be a signal.' Tek's voice floated through the air.

'How will we know what it is?' Grace Peak asked.

'I can assure you, you will know,' came the reply.

Chapter 8

Sacrifice

Tyrone slept surprisingly soundly.

He had the weirdest dream. It started off with him looking in his bedroom mirror. What he saw reflected there was him and yet not him. The boy in the mirror had no weight problem, no protruding teeth and no freckles. He looked older, more heroic.

The dream suddenly switched to a football game, with Tyrone in goals, a new athletic, cat-like Tyrone, who proceeded to execute the most phenomenal dives, deflections and catches to keep his net ball-free.

Then he was sitting at his desk in Class 6M at Rhiwderin Juniors. Bronwyn Spears, the most beautiful girl in the school, was perched on his desk, fluttering her eyelashes at him. She tossed her hair back, bent towards him and whispered in his ear, 'You're stonking, you are!'

'Um, I think you're . . . stonking too,' he replied.

She pouted her lips and said, 'Give us a kiss then, gorgeous.'

Tyrone's heart began to pound, as she bent towards him again, her lips drawing closer, closer . . . GGGGR-RRRRRRAAAAAAAAAAAARRRRRRR!

Tyrone jolted up in his bed. Daphne Gorge was next

to him. All his room mates were in the same, startled, upright position as he was.

'What in tarnation was that?' JW exclaimed.

'I believe that was the signal we've all been waiting for,' said Alpha Minor calmly.

'You mean the game has started?' said Tyrone.

Rufus laughed. 'I was expecting something more subtle.'

'Well,' Grace Peak pointed out, 'it has certainly focused our attention.'

Nobody could argue with that.

They quickly got up. The beds behind them folded up neatly and seemed to devour themselves. Spindle nearly got caught up in his. Eaten by his own bed!

Then, nothing. Nothing happened.

The seven contestants looked at each other, expectantly. One or two began to pace around the room.

What were they supposed to do?

A whole ten minutes passed.

Spindle spoke first. 'How is game played?'

'That's a darn good question there, boy!' JW commented.

More silence, more pacing.

Daphne Gorge was sweating profusely. She sighed, then lay down on the floor. She immediately pointed above her. 'Well, I'll be bumswizzled! Will you look at that?'

There was a screen, floating horizontally, about fifteen metres above their heads. A message was repeatedly scrolling across it in red neon lettering:

GREETINGS ONCE AGAIN, YOUNG CREATURES!

THE OBJECT OF THE GAME IS TO FIND
A CUBE, AN EXACT REPLICA OF THE ONE
YOU ARE NOW INSIDE.

AS THE GAME PROCEEDS, YOUR NUMBERS
WILL DROP MEMBERS OF THE GROUP WILL
DISAPPEAR, ONE BY ONE.

REMEMBER, THERE CAN ONLY BE ONE WINNER!

THE GAME HAS NOW COMMENCED.

MAY THE MOST DESERVING PLANET WIN.

Tyrone glanced around the dormitory. It was a circular room with no furniture or windows or doors, for goodness sake! You couldn't possibly hide a cube in here!

But then the dormitory vanished and, in its place emerged a huge and imposing entrance hall. Tyrone remembered seeing something like it once in a film. The floor was tiled like a chessboard. A futuristic chandelier loomed above them. An escalator with shining metal hand-rails led up to the first landing and then branched left and right and turned back on itself.

Leading off from the entrance hall were six metallic doors, three to the left and three to the right.

JW headed straight for the escalator. 'I'll take upstairs, being as I'm the biggest and the toughest!' he declared. 'You little fellers can take these here doors. And watch out for the Booger-Man!'

'Watch out yourself!' Rufus muttered.

The group started to head off in seven different directions – but didn't get very far.

They were stopped in their tracks by the sound of JW being knocked off his feet by an enormous red carpet which appeared out of nowhere and rolled itself down the escalator treads.

'Jumping Jiggerbites!!!' he yelled, picking himself up and brushing himself down. 'There was no call for that, no call at all!'

The carpet had words woven into it, in black:

We suggest that, during the initial part of the Game,
you all stick together.

Something fell onto Tyrone's head and rolled onto the floor. Rufus picked it up.

It was a scrunched-up ball of paper.

Rufus unfolded it. There was something written on it.

'What is it?' said Tyrone.

Rufus passed it to him. 'See for yourself.'

It was another message:

One final warning.
Watch out for the Vorcansplatter.

'What the heck's a Vorcansplatter?' exclaimed Rufus, scratching one of his horns.

GGGRRRRRRRAAAAAAAAAAARRRRRR!

The chandelier shook in fright.

'I think that may have answered your question,' said Grace Peak.

A violent pounding came from the floor above them. To Tyrone, it sounded like a T-rex running amok up there. It moved quickly from one end of the ceiling to the other and towards the top of the escalator.

Spindle was ricocheting around like a bullet, piping at the top of his voice, 'Don't want to die! Too young!'

Like reluctant gladiators, the seven contestants huddled together. This didn't feel like a game any more.

With a sudden WHOOOOOMP, the Vorcansplatter launched itself onto the landing in front of them.

'Holy cowbags!' Tyrone yelled, in utter disbelief.

Rufus took a sideways glance at Daphne Gorge. 'Boy, and I thought you were scary!'

'Pig!' she responded.

The Vorcansplatter was certainly frightening, by anyone's definition! Try imagining the scary thing under your bed, then double it, triple it even! That should give you some idea.

It was all fangs and claws, slime, slobber and drool.

It was not in a good mood either!

To Tyrone, it looked hungry – in need of fast food and in no mood to hang about for tomato sauce.

He whispered, 'I wonder why it's called a Vorcansplatter.'

'Why don't you go and ask?' Grace Peak suggested.

Rufus Blade was pacing back and forth like a tiger on

a leash. Suddenly, he huffed and puffed and started swaggering towards the bottom of the moving staircase.

'And what precisely does he think he's doing?' Grace Peak said, frowning.

'I don't know,' said Tyrone, wondering why Miss Telepathic didn't already know, 'but I don't like the look of it.'

The young Martian just stood there in front of the Vorcansplatter. They seemed to be engaged in some sort of staring competition.

'Oy, you up there, Dorkansucker, whatever-your-name-is!' he shouted up at it. 'You're making me quake in my boots!'

The Vorcansplatter may not have understood Rufus's words but it obviously picked up on his taunting tone and attitude, because it jolted forward like a revving juggernaut.

'Ooh! Ooh!' Spindle panicked, taking refuge behind JW's huge stripy frame.

Rufus wasn't backing down. He obviously enjoyed living dangerously. 'Oy,' he continued, 'did anybody ever tell you how ugly you are? Have you looked in the mirror recently? The last time I saw anything as ugly as you, it was on the back end of a babooki!'

Tyrone wondered what a babooki was.

The Vorcansplatter took a huge step forwards and shook its gigantic head from side to side, soaking the carpet with purple slobber.

'Take it easy, Rufus,' Tyrone advised from the sidelines.

Alpha Minor, meanwhile, had managed to make his

way over to one of the doors and was quietly beckoning the others towards it.

There was no stopping Rufus – he was on a roll. 'Are you sure your mother didn't drop you on your head?' he enquired of the Vorcansplatter. 'Like, from the top of a mountain!'

The Vorcansplatter's eyes turned a blazing shade of red.

'I think you've gone too fa-ar!' JW sang out.

What happened next was a complete blur.

With an ear-splitting roar, the creature launched through the air towards Rufus. At the same time, Rufus, obviously sensing its intentions, scooted quickly under it and behind it, up the staircase – which had ceased to move!

For a few nerve-shredding seconds, Tyrone and the others found themselves gazing up at the Vorcansplatter's dripping nostrils but then, like five streaks of lightning, they shot through the door which was being held open for them by Alpha Minor.

Spindle spoke for all of them. 'Oooh! Oooh! Oooh! Aaaaaaaargh!!!'

The door was slammed shut. JW promptly positioned his huge backside up against it and the rest of the group huddled up against him.

Tyrone grabbed his asthma inhaler from his pocket and took a quick puff. The game had begun in earnest now.

This was serious. Somebody could be killed!

'Why this particular door?' Grace Peak asked.

'I sensed this was a good way,' said Alpha Minor.

'Well, that must make it OK,' she said, sarcastically. 'You must be our new leader then?'

'That is not my wish,' Alpha stated calmly.

Stretched out in front of the contestants was a long grey curving corridor. Tyrone didn't want to think about what lay in wait for them at the other end of it!

'We can't just leave Rufus out there!' he said.

'He seems to be managing just fine!' declared JW.

Tyrone squeezed behind him and slowly opened the door a few centimetres. He could just make out the rear end of the Vorcansplatter heading back towards the escalator.

Rufus was standing at the top. He had some sort of weapon in his claw, which he must have had concealed in his leather jacket. It looked like a sling-shot, the kind of thing David used to knock out Goliath.

'Head up, Vorky baby!' he yelled, swinging his weapon above his head.

The Vorcansplatter's head comically swung round and round as it focussed on what Rufus was doing.

Then, with incredible speed, Rufus launched his personal missile right towards the creature's snout.There was a deafening roar of pain, and anger, Tyrone guessed, as the Vorcansplatter sank to its knees.

'Oooh, that's gotta hurt!' exclaimed Rufus, surfing down the stair-rail and heading for the door.

'Open up!' he yelled.

Tyrone let him through.

'Where did you all get to?' Rufus said, smirking.

Grace Peak turned away in disgust. 'Some of us have

the good sense to know when to run.' Spindle was hopping from one leg to another, very agitated.

'What's up, buddy? Need the toilet?' Rufus enquired.

'We go now,' he stated, pulling Rufus's hand.

It seemed like a good idea to Tyrone.

'Which way?' Rufus joked.

They headed off down the dimly-lit tunnel, not knowing where they were heading but just glad not to be on the Vorcansplatter's lunch-menu.

Five minutes later, Spindle was still tugging on Rufus's hand.

'Hold on there, little buddy,' JW intervened. 'We're perfectly safe in here. That there Vorcansplatter could never squeeze its huge behind into this itty-bitty tunnel, I can assure you of th . . .'

GGGGGRRRRRAAAAAAAAAARRRRRR!

The roar seemed uncomfortably close.

'Um, that would be some other blummin' monster, would it then?' commented Daphne Gorge, as she squeezed her way rapidly to the front.

Tyrone could feel his heart hammering in his chest. 'I don't understand how it could get through that tiny door?' he said.

The Vorcansplatter, it seemed, was a very flexible beast. Back down the tunnel, a huge, slug-like shadow was shuffling towards them.

This was no time to stand and ponder. Everyone, including Rufus, sped off and ran, flat out, for a good five minutes, until some of them, Tyrone included, had to stop for breath.

Silence back down the tunnel. For a moment anyway.

Then, slurping, gurgling noises!

It was relentless! There was no stopping it!

'I thought you said this was a good way,' Grace Peak muttered accusingly at Alpha Minor.

'I felt sure it was,' he said.

They started running again.

The corridor started to slope downwards more and more steeply, which resulted in a few jostles, even tumbles. And then, it began to veer to the right, more and more and more sharply until . . .

THUNK!!

The running came to an abrupt end!

The contestants at the front found themselves nose-to-nose with a metal wall. Those at the back found themselves on the floor after bouncing off those at the front.

From behind them, slither . . . slobber . . . gargle . . . gurgle . . .

Nobody said a word.

There was nothing left to say.

This was the worst possible scenario.

'Wait . . . a . . . minute . . .' Tyrone mumbled. His lips were pressed up against a button. 'I think this might be a lift.'

'PRESS BUTTON QUICK!!' Spindle screeched, trying to push his way through the other contestants.

Tyrone pressed the 'call' button with his nose.

The door opened instantaneously and they all fell in.

The Vorcansplatter's snout appeared around the bend. Blood was dripping from its three nostrils. When it caught sight of Rufus, it smiled. And it wasn't a 'pleased to meet you' sort of smile, either!

There was a whole array of buttons inside the lift, with letters on them instead of numbers – one for every letter of the alphabet, as far as Tyrone could see.

'PRESS! PRESS! PRESS!' Spindle yelled, virtually climbing over the top of him.

Tyrone pressed the button marked 'B'. He had no idea why! B for Back Home?

'He IS pressing, you SILLY creature!!' Grace Peak screamed, backing up against a wall.

Daphne Gorge was jiggling up and down and her leaves were sweating profusely.

The lift wasn't moving and nor was the Vorcansplatter. Drool slobbered from the corners of its cavernous mouth and mingled with the blood from its nostrils.

This was going to be ugly!

Why wasn't the lift moving??

Then a red light on the ceiling flashed on and off. What now??

A robotic voice, coming from some speakers in the walls, stated, matter-of-factly:

This transporting device is designed to take a maximum weight of 3,000 zoks. It is currently overloaded and will not function until some adjustment is made.

'3,000 socks?' That was what Tyrone had heard. 'What does that mean?'

'Not socks, idiot!' said Grace Peak, losing all patience. 'Zoks! Obviously some unit of measurement.'

'3,000? That's a big number? We can't weigh more than that?' Tyrone said, finding himself staring at JW 'Can we?'

JW shrugged.

'The fact is,' said Rufus, 'we're over the weight limit and we ain't moving.'

The Vorcansplatter took a step forward.

'One of us is going to have to get out,' Grace Peak stated, coldly.

'After you, girlie,' said Rufus.

The Vorcansplatter's face filled the doorway. Tyrone could smell its foul breath. Its growling was making the lift vibrate.

The seven contestants squashed themselves up against the back wall.

'Want Mother,' sobbed Spindle.

Tyrone wanted his too.

Then, with unexpected decisiveness, Alpha Minor stepped forward, wished everyone good luck, pressed the button again and vacated the lift.

'Wait!' Tyrone started to say.

But the lift-doors snapped shut.

Chapter 9

Tender Love and Care

The contestants were shaken by a terrifying thud. A dent appeared in the door. Tyrone heard himself urging the lift to move.

But nothing happened.

'WHY NOT MOVING??!!' yelled Spindle, hopping from foot to foot.

At which point they did start to move. Downwards. Very quickly!

Hearts in mouths, they glued themselves to the lift-walls. Tyrone was having trouble believing what had just happened. Alpha Minor, the dolphin-like creature from Neptune, had sacrificed himself so that Tyrone and the others could survive.

The lift started to slow down. 'There are now six of us left,' Grace Peak announced, 'and Neptune no longer exists.'

Rufus frowned at her in disgust. 'You are one cold piece of work!'

JW tut-tutted. 'That there boy sacrificed himself for us,' he declared, wiping a tear from his pink eye.

Grace Peak turned away from them. 'He didn't have to, did he?'

'I declare,' said JW. 'That's mighty ungrateful of you!

The lift came to an abrupt halt.

Daphne Gorge pushed herself to the back. 'I 'ope there be no more o' them blummin' Vorcansplatters in the basement,' she said, as the doors opened.

It wasn't a basement, though. It was a barn. 'B' stood for 'barn'.

Tyrone stepped out of the lift and found himself in hay, right up to his ankles. The barn had two floors, connected by a rickety-looking ladder.

'Smells just like home!' JW exclaimed, sucking in a deep breath.

Grace Peak turned up her nose and pursed her lips. 'Why do I feel so grateful that I don't live there?'

'The feeling's mutual, I'm sure, little lady.'

Spindle popped out of the lift, looking left and right, then started diving in and out of the hay, leaving a trail of scorch-marks behind him.

'What's he up to?' said Tyrone.

'That's obvious, isn't it?' commented Grace Peak. 'He's looking for the Cube.'

How could he switch from abject fear one minute to ferreting greed the next? Anything could be hidden inside that hay!

But, with a second's thought, the rest of the contestants soon joined him, heading off in every direction.

JW bounded to the upper floor and Rufus wasn't far behind him, scampering up the ladder like a red-skinned chimpanzee.

Visibility soon became a problem as the six contestants began to toss hay this way and that. Tyrone was soon in difficulties. The hay dust was playing havoc with his asthma.

'Do you MIND!!' declared Grace Peak, spitting out a mouthful of uninvited hay.

'Watch where you're putting your blummin' hands!' Daphne Gorge warned Spindle.

After five minutes of frantic and exhausting rummaging, Tyrone felt like giving up. 'This is ridiculous,' he said. 'Talk about looking for a needle in a . . . haystack!'

After a few more minutes, they'd all given up!

The dust began to settle and the contestants could see each other again.

'Pheeeee-eww!' said JW, wiping his brow and plonking himself down on a pile of hay. 'This is thirsty work!'

Then Spindle was off again, darting this way and that. 'Somebody tie him down!' moaned Rufus.

But Spindle was stopped in his tracks anyway. As he ran towards the ladder which connected the two floors of the barn, it suddenly disconnected itself and revolved in the air so that it floated horizontally above them.

'What next?' groaned Rufus.

From underneath the ladder, a large sheet of green canvas unfurled itself, revealing the following message:

YOU WILL NOT FIND THE CUBE IN THE BARN.

Just like that. Then the sheet dropped to the floor.

Then a second sheet of canvas unfurled itself from the ladder.

PLEASE NOTE: ALTHOUGH THE MAIN OBJECT OF THE GAME IS TO FIND THE CUBE, YOU MAY BE REQUESTED, AT VARIOUS STAGES, TO PERFORM CERTAIN TASKS.

YOUR FIRST TASK WILL BE TO CATCH A CHOODLE, FEED IT, GROOM IT AND SHOW IT SOME TLC.

'Some what?' Grace Peak frowned, dusting hay frantically from her silvery robes.

'Tender Loving Care,' explained Tyrone.

'There's probably not much of that where you come from,' Rufus commented.

More green canvas:

YOU WILL EACH BE GRADED OUT OF TEN. THE CONTESTANT WHO RECEIVES THE LOWEST MARK WILL BE ELIMINATED FROM THE GAME.

MARKS WILL BE ALLOCATED BY THE CHOODLES THEMSELVES.

Spindle scratched his head. 'What is choodle?'

'Sounds like *poodle*,' Tyrone observed. 'If they're anything like poodles, this should be easy.'

'What are poodles?' Rufus enquired.

'Well, they're sort of fluffy and cute.'

'So,' Grace Peak scowled, 'not like those things over there, then!' She was pointing beyond Tyrone to a large corral area just visible through the half-open barn-door.

58

Tyrone spun around slowly and gulped. 'Um. No.' What he could see was a group of about six or seven creatures lumbering and clumping around in the corral. Under no possible circumstances could anyone describe them as 'cute'.

'Cute' usually means 'small'! And 'cuddly'.

These creatures were big and anything but cuddly! They had two legs apiece. Big, strong-looking things and bent the wrong way, like ostriches. And at the top were large shaggy pom-poms, each one a different colour and all of them lurid – pink, purple, turquoise, scarlet, mustard, amber . . .

No sign of any eyes, ears, noses or mouths, though!

In fact, no sign of any heads!

Just powerful legs and shaggy pom-poms!

The six contestants gathered together in the barn doorway to get a closer look at the choodles who were lolloping around, some scuttling continually back and forth, others loping around in circles. There were collisions aplenty, some of which looked painful.

'This is going to be fun,' muttered Rufus.

JW stepped forward, paws resting on his hips. 'This couldn't be easier! Why, back on my home planet, my baby sister's got pets bigger than those things!'

Rufus gave this comment a slow hand-clap. 'If it's that easy, why don't you show us what to do?'

JW half-frowned, half-smiled, made a grand gesture of stroking his whiskers and took a huge, confident stride forward towards the manic choodles, who seemed to have picked up their pace while the contestants had been arguing.

'Nothing to it!' JW asserted.

Right on cue, one of the choodles – a purple one – slowed down and came to a halt, right in front of him.

JW held out his paw and made some clicking noises in the roof of his mouth. 'Here boy!' he beckoned.

The choodle edged towards him. 'There's a good boy!' JW said, leaning forward to stroke it. But, before he could touch it, it leapt in the air, let out a squeal and butted him right between the eyes. There must have been something solid inside the pom-pom because it made quite a clunk.

The choodle then scampered off to join the rest of his large, very brightly-coloured family.

JW lay on his back, trying to work out why he could see stars when it wasn't night-time!

Tyrone and Rufus struggled to get him to his feet. A fork-lift truck would have been useful.

'So,' smirked Rufus. 'Nothing to it, eh?'

JW pushed his helpers to one side. 'No fluffy purple pom-pom is going to get the better of me!' he declared, staggering forward for another attempt.

There was a brief moment of hesitation from the other five contestants but then the choodle-chase began in earnest.

The creatures proved very tricky to catch. Many and various methods were used to try and capture them. All unsuccessful.

Spindle tried grabbing hold of a passing leg, but ended up being taken for a ride – a very bumpy ride! Daphne Gorge tried the 'leg' approach too, but kept sliding off.

Rufus's unconventional method was to stand in front of any passing choodles and yell with all his might, hoping to scare them into stopping! He might as well have stood in front of a herd of stampeding cattle!

Tyrone found himself out of breath after two minutes, still not recovered from the hay-search.

Grace Peak stood near the barn-door, arms folded, half-heartedly reaching out for any choodles that happened to run close by.

Then Rufus called out, 'I've got one! I've got one!'

Tyrone glanced over.

Rufus stood face-to-face with a turquoise choodle, holding it tightly with both his claws, in a sort-of judo grip. The choodle pulled against him.

Rufus pulled back.

They jiggled one way. They joggled the other way.

Back and forth. Back and forth.

Then they started to spin round.

Faster and faster and faster . . .

Soon, all you could see was a blur of red, black and turquoise.

'Let GOoo!!!' Tyrone found himself calling out.

And that's exactly what Rufus did, flying through the air like a Martian cannonball, straight into the side of the barn into a large wooden barrel.

He sat there, concussed, arms and legs drooping over the side. It looked like he wouldn't be moving for quite some time but, with a sudden yelp, he shot out of the barrel like a cork from a bottle.

The other contestants gathered round to help pick him up from the floor.

'What's in there?' Tyrone nodded towards the barrel.

'How am I supposed to know,' Rufus mumbled, still looking dazed. 'I haven't got eyes in my backside! Whatever it is, it's prickly.'

'Why dun't one of you big strong fellas go and see what it is?' Daphne Gorge teased.

JW stepped forward. 'I do believe I'll take a peek!' he declared.

He strode over to the barrel and peered cautiously over the rim.

'Stay well back now,' he warned the others, squashing his ample belly up against the side and reaching in. And then he stopped moving.

'Hey!' Rufus called over. 'Are you OK?'

With that, JW let out an almighty yowl and his body started to convulse. 'IT'S GOT ME!' he screamed. 'SOMEBODY HELP ME!'

He dropped to the floor, rolling around as if on fire.

Tyrone didn't know what to do. Running away seemed like a pretty good option.

Then he heard the sound of laughter. JW's laughter.

The large Jupiterian stood up. He was rocking back and forth. 'Fooled y'all!' he called over. He marched over to them, tut-tutting. 'Hey, I notice none of you rushed over to lend any assistance. I guess I know who my friends are!'

Grace Peak looked as if she'd just sucked on a lemon. She shook her head. 'Very amusing, I must say.'

JW was holding something.

'What's that?' Tyrone asked.

He held it up. 'It's a brush. A grooming brush. That there barrel's full of 'em.'

'I knew something was prickly,' said an even redder-than-usual Rufus Blade.

While they were talking, one of the choodles went pelting, headfirst, into the side of the barn, causing one of the doors to swing open, revealing a second barrel, exactly the same size and shape as the first one.

'I wonder what's in that one,' said Tyrone.

JW swaggered over to it, followed by the others. They peered over the rim.

'What . . . are . . . those?' frowned Grace Peak. 'I think . . . I feel sick.'

The barrel was alive with tiny white worm-things: a seething mass of wriggling and squiggling movement.

Spindle stood on his black crispy toes and peered over the rim of the barrel. He shook his head from side to side and let out a hiss. 'Don't like squiggles,' he decided.

'You don't like anything,' muttered Rufus.

'They're not squiggles; they're maggots,' said Tyrone.

'I understand the brushes,' said Rufus, 'but what are the maggots for?'

'Food?' suggested Daphne Gorge, licking her pink lips.

'Food?' Rufus Blade ranted. 'I ain't eating those! No way! Planet or no planet!'

'Not for us, blockhead,' said Grace Peak, pointing at the choodles. 'For them! We're supposed to groom them and feed them, are we not?'

The choodles continued to lollop around.

JW scooped up a handful of maggots and headed out into the middle of the corral. 'Here, boy!' he started to call out again. 'Here, boy!'

Immediately, an amber-coloured choodle went up to him. A large fleshy black tongue materialized from somewhere inside the hairy mop and snatched up the maggots from JW's paw.

Tyrone had no problem with squiggly things – he'd been fishing with Terry lots of times. He grabbed a large handful from the barrel and set off in search of a hungry choodle.

Daphne Gorge unzipped her stomach and filled herself up with maggots! She could eat anything and looked like she often did!

Rufus, normally brave, seemed to have a problem. After some deliberation, he closed his eyes and, very, very hesitantly, dipped his claw into the barrel, all the time muttering under his breath. Some Martian swear-words no doubt.

Meanwhile, Spindle was hopping up and down in a serious state of agitation. When he saw that the others had a good head-start on him, he swiftly reached over into the barrel, launching a handful of 'squiggles' straight into the air, showering them all over the floor. Surprisingly, this proved quite effective. He was soon surrounded by choodles.

Grace Peak rolled up one of her silver sleeves and, very gingerly, pulled out one wriggling maggot! She screwed up her pointy nose. She held the maggot as far away from her body as possible and headed out into the corral. A passing pink choodle swooped through the air, nimbly snatched the maggot from her fingers and promptly ran off.

And suddenly, like robots that had been switched off, the choodles stopped feeding and sank to the ground. They lay motionless, like huge discarded mops.

'Looks like they've had enough,' Rufus said.

'What now?' said Tyrone.

'I would say, after all that bouncing around,' said JW, 'that they need grooming. Grab some brushes!'

Tyrone picked up a brush from the barrel and knelt in front of a mustard-coloured choodle. He was hoping the creature was going to co-operate. He started brushing and was surprised to find that, when he pushed aside some of the hair on the middle of its body, a face appeared, or part of a face. It was cute, in a baby-troll kind of way.

To everyone's relief, the choodles seemed to love being groomed. Gentle purring sounds vibrated around the corral in an atmosphere of calm and harmony. Tyrone felt himself nodding off.

But the peace was suddenly interrupted as a hidden speaker buzzed into action:

THE TASK IS NOW COMPLETE.

The choodles got to their feet. They arranged themselves so that one of them was standing next to each contestant.

CONTESTANTS, YOUR SCORES WILL NOW BE INDICATED BY THE CHOODLES.

'The choodles? I'd like to see how they're gonna do that!' Rufus declared.

MISS GRACE PEAK FROM SATURN.

The choodle standing alongside her tapped its left foot five times.

YOU GAINED FIVE MARKS OUT OF TEN.
WELL DONE!

JW pointed a finger at Rufus. 'I guess that answers your question, buddy.'
Five didn't seem like a good score to Tyrone.

MISS DAPHNE GORGE FROM VENUS.

Six taps.

SIX MARKS OUT OF TEN. CONGRATULATIONS!

Daphne looked pleased with herself, like she'd just won a Christmas hamper in a raffle. Grace Peak, on the other hand, looked very put out to be beaten by a plant.
And so it went on . . . Rufus scored seven points. Spindle scored six. JW got an amazing nine!
Tyrone was starting to worry. His was the only score that hadn't been announced. If he came last, it'd be goodbye Mum, goodbye Dad, goodbye Wales, goodbye World.

AND LASTLY . . .

Tyrone didn't like the sound of 'lastly'!

TYRONE DAVIES FROM PLANET EARTH.

Here goes . . .

The mustard-coloured choodle next to him started tapping its foot:

One . . . Two . . . Three . . . Four . . . Five – Tyrone's heart nearly stopped – Six . . . Seven . . .Eight.

EIGHT OUT OF TEN.

Phew! Not last, then! Tyrone could have yelled with relief but he was trying to put himself in Grace Peak's shoes. What was going to happen now? This was serious stuff!

The speaker burst back into life.

AS MISS PEAK HAS THE LOWEST SCORE, SHE WILL NOW BE ELIMINATED.

Grace Peak started backing towards the barn. She seemed to have turned an even paler shade of white than normal.

Eliminated? Not a nice word. *Gangsters eliminate people*, thought Tyrone. He was puzzled. If he was to have any chance of winning the game, he needed to know how it worked.

Had Grace Peak just been eliminated because she

wasn't very kind? Was that how it worked? If you have a flaw in your personality, you get eliminated. Tyrone was starting to worry. You'd need to be perfect to win this thing and he knew he was far from that!

The choodles started to shunt the other contestants out of the way as they headed towards the unfortunate loser. She continued backing away but more of them appeared behind her. She was surrounded.

For one terrible minute, Tyrone thought they were going to suffocate her but instead, they rubbed themselves up against her affectionately.

MISS PEAK WILL STAY WITH THE CHOODLES UNTIL THE GAME IS OVER.

Grace Peak smiled with relief. None of the others had ever seen her smile. She looked beautiful, radiant almost! She started stroking and caressing the choodles and they responded with loud purrs.

JW, Rufus, Daphne Gorge, Spindle and Tyrone gathered together near the barn-doors.

'Now what happens to us?' enquired Spindle.

With that, a circular hole opened in the ground beneath them and swallowed them up.

Chapter 10

Meanwhile

Meanwhile, back in the rest of the Solar System . . .

Exactly one hour after Tyrone and the other contestants had 'vanished', Tek made an appearance on TV channels and other communication devices throughout the solar system. He announced, matter-of-factly, that the seven contestants, now identified, were inside the Cube and that the game had commenced. There was nothing anybody could do but wait for the outcome.

Naturally, the news was of concern to Tyrone's family, but they were also relieved he was still alive. Rhodri Lloyd's dad said that Tyrone had just vanished. One moment he was diving for the ball, the next he was gone. The match had to be abandoned.

Tyrone's dad was surprisingly calm and confident, 'That boy has hidden reserves. If anybody can do it, he can.'

'Well I hope they don't ask him to do anything too physical,' said his mum. 'His asthma will play up. I hope he remembered to take his inhaler with him.'

Her husband gave her a reassuring hug.

'And I hope he's wearing a vest,' interjected Nan. 'I bet it's blinkin' cold out there in Space.'

'He was wearing a vest and a pair of thermals under his tracksuit,' said Terry. 'I told him to dress up warm for the match.'

'Well, what a palaver!' declared Mrs Phillips who had invited herself to tea. 'Who would have thought it!'

Joshua Maybry was in his bedroom, trying his best to kick a hole in his wall. Of all the people to choose, they picked Tyrone Davies! He couldn't understand the logic of it. As far as he was concerned, it was goodbye Earth!

Throughout the rest of Wales, reactions varied, but split mainly into two camps.

The optimists carried on with their normal schedules, eating their meals, going to work, following their exercise routines. This was a temporary blip, they felt, and life would soon return to normal.

The pessimists, on the other hand, decided to make the most of what could be their last few moments alive and went wild, partying and holidaying and generally making a nuisance of themselves.

There was a third camp, neither optimists nor pessimists. They sat, motionless, in their armchairs, not quite sure what to do . . .

Chapter 11

Sand-witches on the Beach

The breath was being sucked out of Tyrone. Too scared even to scream, he just clenched his teeth, closed his eyes and prayed. It was pitch-black and they were hurtling at breakneck speed down some sort of helter-skelter. At first, he thought they might all die, but surely that would defeat the object of the whole game. All he could do was wait for the nightmare to end. But it didn't.

They kept right on falling. Seemingly for miles.

Tyrone didn't understand how the Cube could be so big. Yes, it looked big from the outside, but not this big! Perhaps they'd fallen out of it. He couldn't see any stars, though. *Perhaps it's like Doctor Who's Tardis*, he thought – *a lot larger on the inside than the outside.*

Although Tyrone wasn't counting, minutes seemed to pass and the journey wasn't getting any slower! Then there was a blinding blue light, the slide disappeared from under them and they corkscrewed into Space.

Tyrone was treading air and flailing his arms like a windmill. He looked down. They were heading for a huge mass of water.

'Don't like thiiiiiiiiisss!' screeched Spindle as he plummeted like a falling meteorite.

'Tell us something neeeeeeewwwwwww!' Rufus yelled.

One at a time, in rapid succession, the contestants hit the water. Splish!!! Splash!!!! KerSPLOOSH!!!!! JW surfaced first, like a huge inflatable. The others, Tyrone included, popped up around him.

'Hold onto me, all of you!' he offered. 'I have natural buoyancy!'

Tyrone and the others made their way over to their floating friend, coughing and spluttering, and grabbed a limb each.

They appeared to be in an ocean! There was an island a few hundred metres in front of them, a tropical island, palm trees, a beach, the whole works, except that the sky was emerald in colour, the water amber and the sand amethyst.

Tyrone had no idea where all this had come from. It was hard to believe that they were still somewhere inside a cube, floating out in Space. The clear green sky above them seemed to go on forever. Tyrone, despite being able to hold on to JW, was still managing to swallow some salty water. 'What was that?' he called out, feeling something touch his leg.

'What was what?' Rufus said.

'It felt like something just brushed past my leg.'

'You're imagining things, buddy. Chill out. Let's head for shore.'

They all started paddling.

'Well,' declared Daphne Gorge, who had now taken on the appearance of a large piece of seaweed, 'I don't suppose things can get much blummin' worse.'

'Don't say that,' said Tyrone, nervously.

'Will you stop it!' Rufus glared at him. 'You're starting to make me ner . . . What's that?'

'What's what?' they all said.

'THAT!!' he yelled, pointing at four large, pink fins which were slicing through the amber water towards them, just metres away. The fins suddenly veered to the left and started to circle them.

The shore looked a long way away. What were those things! If they were sharks, then they were a funny colour! Whatever colour they were, they were too close for comfort and closing in fast!

Tyrone closed his eyes and thought of home back in Rhiwderin: his mum making him cheese on toast, his nan talking to Tweety-Pie . . .

Something bumped against his stomach. He opened his eyes to find a pink snout and a remarkable set of teeth looking up at him. Not particularly sharp teeth, but perfectly formed, pearly-white and sparkly.

The jaws opened and a female voice chirped, 'Well, hello there!'

One by one, three other pink snouts broke the surface, smiled broadly and delivered friendly greetings:

'How are you?'

'Nice to see you!'

'What a pleasant surprise!'

Then, with perfectly synchronized movements, they submerged themselves again.

Rufus looked as confused as Tyrone felt. 'Somebody please tell me,' he said, 'did that really just happen?'

Before they could fully recover, the pink snouts

reappeared. 'Have a nice day!' called out the first, dazzling them with its beaming smile.

This was followed by choruses of 'See you later!' and 'Missing you already!' before they all disappeared again. Throughout all of this, JW had stayed pretty calm and unbothered.

'Say, dude,' said Rufus, almost admiringly, 'you've been acting pretty cool.'

JW tilted his head slightly. 'Yup, well, I've seen those critters before. We have them back on my planet – only a lot bigger of course.'

'Of course.'

'They're called Sharlenes. They're automata. Their sole purpose is to make your day out an experience never to forget.'

'I've just had an experience I'll never forget!' said Tyrone, whose heartbeat was struggling to return to its regular rhythm.

'No, their job is, well, to be . . . charming.'

'Oh.'

Slowly but surely, JW brought them all to dry land.

The contestants flopped down onto the beach, like wet fish. Once they'd recovered their composure, they were able to appreciate the splendour of the island. Purple sands caressed by lapping amber waves.

Tyrone lay back and soaked in the warmth and beauty.

'Hey! Over here!' Rufus was calling out. 'There's a sign or something!'

Up they all got and headed off towards him, their feet, paws, claws and tendrils trailing strange patterns in the sand.

In an area separated from the rest of the beach by a low clump of turquoise vegetation, Tyrone could just make out the back of a large wooden sign.

'What do you think it says?' Daphne Gorge asked.

'*Sandpit*, probably,' said Rufus.

But it didn't. As the group came around towards it, they saw just three words: **CUBE IN HERE.**

At the base of the signpost lay five large spades. Faster than a chameleon's tongue, Spindle snatched up one of them, leapt into the sandpit and started digging, as if his life depended on it.

'Hmmm,' said JW, paws on hips, gawping at the little creature in front of him, spraying them all with sparkling amethyst sand. 'I suppose we'd better join him, before he goes and finds the darn thing.'

'Or buries the rest of us in sand!' Tyrone commented.

'I blummin' 'ate sand!' declared Daphne Gorge, reluctantly grabbing a spade. 'It gets into every crease and fold!' She had a lot of creases and folds.

The contestants found a spot each and started the excavation. At first they dug slowly. The last few hours had been pretty hectic and energy was in short supply. But the more they dug, the faster they got. There were coughs and splutters aplenty as the sparkling purple grains began to fly into the atmosphere, and the occasional clunk as the odd spade connected with the odd head!

Tyrone remembered the bickering that took place in the barn and now it was all being repeated and intensified.

'Watch what you're doing!'

'This is my spot! Push off!'

'How much of a blummin' spot do you want?'

Things were not going well! And then things went from bad to plain bizarre! One moment Tyrone was scooping away as fast as his muscles and the heavy spade would allow; the next moment, the spade had gone and he was looking at a small spoon in his hand.

And at that very same instant a strange cackling sound erupted from behind him.

Everyone stopped digging.

All the spades had gone. JW now held a feather, Rufus a lolly, Daphne was looking at a microphone and Spindle had a banana. Before the contestants had time to reflect on how ridiculous they felt, the purple sand beneath them turned into mud – the kind of mud that a hippo would feel at home in.

An unseen voice screeched. 'You'll have to keep digging or you'll never win!' More cackling.

Tyrone strained to see who it was.

Three ancient figures, half-hidden by the vegetation, dressed in rags and covered in grime, were lurking in the turquoise undergrowth.

JW threw his feather into the sand. 'My, my, you shouldn't be playing pranks like that at your age!' he called over to them. 'It's about time you grew up!'

The gnarled trio looked at each other and hooted with laughter. One of them said, 'Did you hear that? He says we should grow up.'

The cackling became louder and more uncontrolled. The creatures suddenly started growing taller and taller, until their heads were the same height as the fungus trees in the grove behind them.

They were a pretty scary sight now that they'd been enlarged – straggles of hair, huge warty noses, nearly toothless smiles. And now about five metres tall!

'Are we grown up enough for you now?' they teased, taking a few strides forward.

The contestants took a few nervous steps backwards. 'What have you blummin' done now?' Daphne Gorge muttered, nearly slipping over.

JW shrugged.

'Don't like them,' said Spindle, taking refuge behind Tyrone.

'What a surprise!' said Rufus.

JW plucked up some courage and walked towards the visitors. He bowed. 'Do you think you youngsters could give us our sand back, please?'

Tyrone was amazed by their reaction.

'Oooooh!' declared the leader. 'Did you hear that? Young are we? How charming!'

Tyrone watched in horror as their faces began to change shape. It was as if they were made of rubber. They metamorphosised into younger versions of themselves. Not very attractive, but young, nevertheless.

JW spoke again. 'We'd be real grateful if you beautiful young creatures would kindly consider restoring our sandpit to its former state.'

'Beautiful young creatures!'

'Ooooooooooh! Beautiful now, is it?'

And suddenly, they were, well, nearly beautiful! Eye-catching, certainly. They wouldn't have looked out of place in a gallery of modern art. The newly-beautiful creatures preened themselves.

The leader waved one of her upper limbs, chanting:
'With a wave of my flipper and flick of my hand
Slushy old mud turn back into sand!'
The sand re-materialised.

'Thanks,' said Rufus. 'Now buzz off.'

The giant creatures disappeared and were immediately replaced by three enormous bumblebees, which headed towards the contestants, causing them to dive headfirst into the sand. They then buzzed off up the coastline.

Within seconds, Spindle started jumping up and down like an over-excited chimpanzee.

'FOUND IT! FOUND IT!'

He was waving something.

'I don't believe it,' muttered Rufus, falling to his knees.

'FOUND THE CUBE!'

Tyrone's heart sank. 'Let's have a look,' he said, reaching out.

'No!' yelped Spindle, clasping it to his charcoal chest, like a baby. 'MY cube! MY cube!'

'We only want to see the darn thing!' JW protested.

Spindle held it out in front of him. 'Look!' he said, holding it out quickly and snatching it away even more quickly. And then he scampered off with it, holding it aloft like a winning lottery ticket. He didn't seem at all concerned about the fate of the other planets and their inhabitants.

Once he'd achieved a safe distance from the others, he knelt down in the sand, clutching the cube to his chest. It sounded to Tyrone like he was talking to himself. 'Lovely cube. Pretty cube. MY cube.'

Tyrone, Rufus, JW and Daphne Gorge collapsed in despair onto the sand. Mercury had won the game! It didn't seem fair or logical!

'I sure as heck don't believe this!' JW said, punching the sand. 'If all the creatures on Mercury are like that little feller, it must be a pretty darn selfish planet and they don't deserve to win this here competition!'

A gloomy silence enveloped them.

Tyrone felt like screaming and crying, but it wouldn't solve anything.

'I wonder how long we've got left?' pondered Rufus as the ground beneath them began to shudder. Grains of purple sand started to dance about.

The contestants watched as the amethyst grains became a fountain which grew and grew until there emerged from inside it . . . an enormous yellow crystal.

'A golden rhombohedron,' said JW.

'It's hollow!' said Tyrone. 'It's a container of some kind.'

There was something inside. It looked like a scroll.

'What now?' said Rufus.

'We need to read it,' said Tyrone.

They placed their shoulders up against the side of the rhombohedron and shoved with all their might until it toppled over. Then they lifted the base until one of the faces slid open and the scroll slipped out onto the sand. They unfurled it, Tyrone kneeling on one end and Daphne sitting on the other.

JW read aloud the message, which looked as if it had been written with a very large quill:

TO WHOM IT MAY CONCERN

*THERE WAS **A** CUBE IN THE SANDPIT.*

*BUT NOT **THE** CUBE.*

SPINDLE WILL BE SPENDING SOME TIME HERE ALONE, WITH JUST HIS CUBE FOR COMPANY. GOOD LUCK TO THE FOUR REMAINING CONTESTANTS!

This was starting to make sense. It seemed logical that Spindle should be eliminated. He had to be the most selfish being Tyrone had ever met. He didn't give a second's thought to the needs of others. It was a case of Me, me, me!

And now he was Gone, gone, gone!

Chapter 12

Moo-tang Rescue

A familiar flicker woke Tyrone and the remaining three contestants.

The island vanished and, almost as if someone was using a remote-control to switch channels, a forest took its place. Huge trees loomed above them. Shafts of sunlight struggled to fight their way through.

It was all very calm, very tranquil, almost magical.

And yet too calm, too tranquil.

Spindle, if he'd been there, would probably have found something not to like about it. But the silence was abruptly disturbed by the sound of movement from above.

Rufus looked up just in time to avoid being hit by a seedcase the size of a small pineapple.

Tyrone bent down to pick it up. 'Look! It's got writing on it!' Somebody had scraped a word into the shiny outer skin.

Daphne Gorge rested her chin on his arm. 'What do it say?'

'It says OPEN.'

Rufus grabbed the seedcase out of Tyrone's hands and split it with his razor-sharp nails.

A pair of what looked like crumpled-up sweet wrappers dropped to the floor. Rufus picked one up and uncrumpled it. There was one word written on it: LOOKING.

Daphne passed the other wrapper to him. The word this time was: START.

'Looking start?' Rufus said, frowning and scratching his left horn.

JW coughed. 'I think you'll find that it's *Start looking*.'

Tyrone spun himself around slowly. They had to be kidding!

Looking for the Cube? Here? It could be anywhere: at the top of a tree, behind a bush, behind a leaf!

Daphne Gorge threw herself to the ground. 'I give up!' she protested, lying on her belly and thrashing out with her legs. 'I'm starvin' an' I wanna go HOME!!'

Rufus kicked a twig. 'I ain't searching,' he said defiantly.

Tyrone didn't feel like moving either. He stood quite still, soaking in the atmosphere of the glade – the pure air, the shafts of sunlight caressing his skin.

'If only life could be like this all the time,' mused JW. 'No rushing around chasing your tail, no stress, no arguing or fighting . . .'

Such peace. Such quiet. And then a phone rang.

The sound seemed to be coming from inside the enormous tree behind them. Its trunk must have been two metres wide at the base.

The phone was persistent.

As Tyrone circled the tree, he came face to face with a telephone box – an old-fashioned, heavy-duty telephone kiosk like the one in Mr Evans's garden at the end of Tredegar Street.

The phone kept on ringing.

As nobody wanted to miss out on anything important, the four of them crammed themselves into the box. It was a very tight squeeze!

Rufus picked up the phone. 'Yup?'

'Young creatures . . .' a voice began.

'Well, well, if it isn't old bulldog-features!'

'Yes, yes, highly amusing I'm sure, young Master Rufus. Many congratulations on reaching this stage of the competition. You will be allowed a short respite from your search. Meanwhile, a new task awaits you. At the end of it, three of you will remain.'

There was a groan from the back of the telephone kiosk. 'What's he saying?' Daphne Gorge struggled to make herself heard. 'I can't hear a blummin' thing. I'm stuck here under somebody's cheek!' She was referring to JW's huge behind, which was squashing her up against the glass.

'We've got another task.'

'Oh. Well, let's get on with it, then!'

Rufus put the phone back to his ear and frowned. He banged the phone on the glass. 'I don't believe it. He's gone.'

'What's the task, then?' Daphne Gorge enquired.

'He didn't say.'

'Blummin' wonderful!' said Daphne, squeezing her face free. 'Not only do we have to find the Cube but now we have to guess the blummin' task! Absolutely blummin' marvellous!'

Tyrone had to agree.

Rufus slammed the phone back down into its cradle.

A voice called out from above the telephone box. 'Hellooooooo!'

It sounded as if someone was stuck up a tree.

There was a sudden thump from above and an upside-down head peered in at them from the top of the box. Not an unpleasant-looking face. But green!

'All right in there, are we?' enquired the head. Daphne Gorge pushed against the door and they all tumbled out in a heap.

With the skill of a trained gymnast, the figure attached to the head flipped off the top of the telephone box and landed in front of them.

He was quite strikingly handsome, with a moustache and goatee beard and hair tied back in a pony-tail. But his skin and hair were green. He looked human and yet not human. His ears were strangely pointed and he had an earring in one of them.

He reached down and helped the contestants to their feet. Rubbing his hands together, he declared, 'Right, boys and girls – and plants, of course! I am in need of your assistance. I've got a big job on today. Can't possibly do it on my own. What do you say?'

He had a charming, persuasive manner, with a smile wider than the Pacific Ocean and teeth that could dazzle you from a hundred paces.

JW looked confused. 'Who exactly are you, fella?' he asked.

The green man's smile grew even wider. 'I have many names. To some I am known as Zedulon Gallant; to others I am known as Captain Zed; to others I am the Redistributor.'

'The Redistributor?' frowned Rufus.

Zed nodded. 'There are some who have just have too much in life and yet others have nothing at all. My mission, as I see it, is to even up the balance a bit. So I redistribute things.'

Like Robin Hood, thought Tyrone, *or Twm Siôn Cati*. 'So what do you want us to do?' he asked.

'Help me free some moo-tang,' he said. 'They'll be passing this way within the hour.'

'What's blummin' moo-tang?' Daphne asked. She sounded impatient. Probably hungry again, Tyrone decided!

'Moo-tang are animals, my flower,' Captain Zed explained. 'Very rare and precious. They're talented little creatures. They give milk and eggs; they can do the work of ten men; they're faithful, they're loyal and, if you treat them well, they can live for over a hundred years.'

'Who are we rescuing them from?' asked Tyrone.

'Porco the Hideous.'

'Sounds like a nice character.'

'Hmmmm. He has a nasty habit of kidnapping moo-tang and demanding ransoms from their owners.'

'So,' Rufus said, trying to clarify the situation, 'you want us to steal some moo-tang from this Porky character and then give them back to some poor people.'

'Exactly right!' declared Zed, whacking Rufus on the back. 'Only I wouldn't call it stealing. I don't really see how you can steal from thieves, do you? So then, are you going to help?'

It was difficult to say no to someone with such a winning way about him. If his smile had been any bigger, it would have fallen off!

'Now, if you three will just close your eyes, this will only take a jiffy.'

'Close our eyes?' said Rufus, defensively. 'Why?'

'Look, just trust me.'

'Hold on there, dude,' said Rufus. 'I don't trust anybody that I've only known five minutes!'

Captain Zed placed his hands on his hips and gave a hearty laugh. 'Look, I promise this won't hurt, as long as you close your eyes,' he said, reaching round behind his back, whipping out a can of goodness-knows-what, quickly shaking it and spraying it all over them.

By the time he'd finished, they were a beautiful shade of green.

'You are now officially members of the Green Resistance!' he declared, stepping back to admire his artwork.

Daphne was looking decidedly dejected.

Zed crouched down in front of her, tapping her fronds. 'Don't feel left out, my flower. Don't you think you look green enough already? It's only for camouflage, anyway.'

Daphne actually blushed.

Rufus was clearly not impressed with his new colour-scheme. 'Was this absolutely necessary? I don't see why we couldn't have hidden behind a tree or something.'

Tyrone had to laugh. Green was not Rufus's colour!

'I don't know what you're laughing at,' said Rufus, 'You haven't seen what you look like!'

JW looked more hilarious than both of them put together! A big green balloon-cat!

Their new leader dropped suddenly to the forest floor and placed his ear to the ground. 'Someone's coming! Quick! Get over behind that bush!'

Rufus looked completely dumbfounded. 'Behind a bush? Am I missing something? Will someone please tell me why I've just been sprayed with green paint?' he muttered, following the others behind a bush the size of a small house.

'Ssshhhh!'

'Don't tell me to ssshhh! I'm covered in sticky, smelly green gunge and I have no idea why!'

A rumbling could be heard and the ground was shaking.

A procession rolled into view: six soldiers on humped creatures. Rather like camels, Tyrone decided. The 'camels' were followed by an open carriage followed by six more mounted soldiers followed by a covered wagon. Sitting in the front of the open carriage was an enormous and repulsive-looking creature. He had a pig's snout, tusk-like teeth, long coarse greying hair and a pair of sideburns a werewolf would have been proud of. In his right hand was a fly-swatter.

Tyrone was starting to have serious doubts. 'I don't understand how we're supposed to get the moo-tang, whatever they are, away from that thing,' he whispered, 'never mind about the twelve soldiers.'

'Where are the blummin' moo-tang?' enquired Daphne.

'In there,' said Captain Zed, pointing to the large covered wagon. 'Listen. I'll create a diversion while you lot creep around the back of the wagon and grab two moo-tang a-piece.'

'Two?' whispered Tyrone.

Before anybody could stop him, their new leader strode off towards the oncoming procession and brought it to an abrupt halt. You could almost hear the screech of brakes.

He just stood there, hands on hips, bold as brass. 'Good day to you, my fine fellows!' he declared with disarming breeziness.

'Wadda you want?' said the lead rider, looking confused.

'Your help, if you would be so kind.'

He took a few more steps towards the riders and lowered his voice to a conspiratorial whisper. 'You see, I am a treasure hunter. My current quest is for the gold at the end of the rainbow. You see that huge rainbow up there?' He pointed heavenwards. Magically, the six soldiers and the six camel-like creatures they were sitting on looked up in the same direction.

'Well, as you can see, the one end of it disappears into that clearing.'

Twelve heads followed his arm obediently.

'You may find this hard to believe but I have just uncovered a huge pot of gold in there behind those trees. But it's too heavy for me to carry on my own . . .'

Straining to hear, the six soldiers at the rear made their way to the front. Porco the Hideous lurched forward in his seat.

The lead rider twisted around in his saddle. 'Shall we do him some damage, Your Hideousness?'

Porco swatted some more flies. He looked pensive. He stared at the irritating green man in front of him.

Finally, he growled, 'I knows you.'

'Can't see how,' came the swift reply.

Further staring.

'Yes I do. You're that Redistributor bloke. The one that steals from hard-working people like me and gives to lazy good-for-nothings.'

'I'm sorry. You've got me mixed up with some other fella,' said Captain Zed, backing away and gesturing to Tyrone and the others. 'It happens to me all the time.'

The newly initiated members of the Green Resistance crawled out from behind the bush and scurried towards the back of the covered wagon.

'I have to admit,' Zed continued, 'I've heard of this Redistributor bloke. But, I can assure you, I would never dream of stealing from you. Now look at me while I tell you about this pot of gold deep, deep in the woods. Look into my eyes. Think of falling down a golden tunnel, falling, falling, so far that you feel drowsy . . . so sleeeepy . . .'

Tyrone couldn't believe it. Zed was sending them into some sort of hypnotic trance. He and the other contestants quickly set about their mission.

JW pulled a cover from off the back of the wagon.

Cramped inside the cage, in a pitiful state, were twenty or so moo-tang – much smaller creatures than Tyrone had imagined them to be, bright orange and very closely resembling orangutangs, apart from the fact that they had udders!

There were about five locks on the cage door. Tyrone was just wondering how they were going to get the moo-tang out when JW squeezed his two not inconsiderable arms through the bars of the cage. While the others looked on in astonishment, he closed his eyes, puffed and strained until his arms started to inflate. The bars of the cage groaned and creaked until they began to bend outwards. He kept right on straining, his arms increasing in size, the bars bending further and further apart until two decently-sized gaps had been created.

At once, JW's arms returned to their normal size. He turned round. 'Sometimes I just downright amaze myself!' he declared. 'Let's go get us some moo-tang.'

But, as he removed his arms from the bars, pandemonium ensued! The moo-tang escaped in a blur of udders and orange fur. Clearly excited to be free, they became living whirlwinds, twisting and spinning their way round bushes, under horses, up trees, in and out of wheels.

The soldiers were violently roused from their trance by the manically twirling creatures. Some were knocked senseless. One tried to grab a passing moo-tang but nearly ended up wrapped around himself!

Rufus, not having learned anything from his encounter with the choodles, ended up first dancing with a moo-tang and then being slam-dunked into a bird's nest.

Daphne Gorge found herself hanging from a branch like some exotic fungus.

With most of their numbers down, the three soldiers who remained conscious decided to cut their losses and run. Angry and bewildered, Porco the Hideous sat in the very centre of this madness. 'Come back, you louts!' he called after his men.

Discarding his fly-swatter, he stood up, now waving a sword in one hand and an axe in the other. He swung them round in desperation but failed to see the moo-tang which, in the process of rebounding off a tree, smacked straight into his back and sent him sailing, very ungracefully, through the air. A camel's rear end brought his journey to an abrupt and undignified halt.

Tyrone had taken refuge behind a tree-trunk and was waiting for the storm to die down.

And, after a few minutes, that's what happened.

The pace of the moo-tang slackened, like toys whose batteries had run out. Eventually, they were reduced to walking pace, with their long arms dragging on the forest floor. If Tyrone didn't know any better, he'd have said they'd been tranquillised. As a result, they put up no struggle and the newly-qualified members of the Green Resistance were able to round them up, two a-piece.

Captain Zed swiftly hog-tied Porco with some of his own rope and then stood up, it seemed, to address the trees. 'Is anybody out there? You can come out now. The danger's over!'

The contestants watched in amazement as what looked like a whole village of tired and starving people emerged from the trees, shrubs and bushes. Green people!

The declaration continued. 'Thanks to my brave young friends here, you now have enough moo-tang to provide you with food for the winter. You might want to show them your appreciation.'

An enormous cheer erupted from the villagers. This was followed by waves of hand-shaking, back-slapping and even kissing.

Tyrone handed over a pair of sleeping moo-tang, as did Rufus and JW. Daphne, however, only had one to offer the villagers.

Tyrone glanced around. 'Where's the other one?'

'Yeah,' added Rufus. 'You definitely had two.'

Daphne shuffled from side to side. 'It – um – got away,' she mumbled, her eyes fixed firmly on the floor.

Tyrone noticed that Daphne's belly seemed to be performing some exotic dance. It was moving from side to side.

Surely not, he thought.

'Quick!' Rufus shouted. 'Open her up! She's eaten one!'

Daphne found herself pinned to the floor. The two sections of her belly were prised apart and out popped an unfortunate moo-tang, clearly the worse-for-weather, its orange fur dripping with digestive juices. It threw Daphne a murderous look.

'I said I was 'ungry,' blubbered Daphne, 'but nobody was blummin' listening to me. Sorry!'

Her sobs were interrupted by the phone ringing again.

Tyrone was the nearest to it, so he ran over to the telephone box.

The others watched as he entered, picked up the phone, nodded a few times, put the phone back down and then exited again.

'What's happening, dude?' enquired Rufus.

'That was Tek,' explained Tyrone. 'He says that you, me and JW are to get in the phone box now and that we have successfully completed this phase of the competition.' Tyrone had known what the message would be. Daphne had let her stomach rule her heart and head. And now she must pay the price.

'What about me?' Daphne sobbed, sitting up and re-assembling her mid-section.

'Sorry, Daphne,' Tyrone said. 'Only us three. Tek said you're to stay here.'

Daphne struggled to her feet. 'But I said I was sorry. I can't help being blummin' 'ungry, can I?'

Captain Zed put his arm around her. 'Don't fret, my flower!' he comforted. 'As you are now an honorary member of my gang, you will be made very welcome here . . .'

Daphne was inconsolable and collapsed in a blubbering heap.

'. . . The moo-tang will make sure you are more-than-well provided-for with grub.'

At the mention of food, the blubbering stopped and a hint of a smile appeared.

So then there were three – JW, Rufus and Tyrone.

Who was going to win? Who should win? Was Tyrone more deserving than the other two? He could see their weaknesses: JW was a bit full of himself; Rufus was quick to lose his temper.

But he had faults of his own. Daphne didn't have a monopoly on greed. He was quite greedy himself. And lazy! When was the last time he made his own bed? Or did the washing-up?

Chapter 13

El Diablo

After saying their farewells, the three remaining contestants squeezed themselves back inside the telephone box, which seemed to have become smaller since the last time they'd been in it.

'This sure is some tight fit,' commented JW, elbowing Tyrone in the ear. 'You and me ain't exactly no beanpoles!'

Tyrone didn't need reminding about his size. He felt sorry for poor Rufus having to share this cramped space with JW and himself.

The telephone box started to shake and shudder violently. There was a tremendous WHOOOOSH and the box shot like a rocket into the air. Within two seconds, the trees below them resembled small clumps of broccoli.

'Don't like thi-iiis!' joked Rufus, echoing Spindle.

Tyrone was reminded of a book he'd once read in school about a glass elevator but Rhiwderin Juniors and books seemed a long way away now.

Wherever they were heading, it surely couldn't be any stranger than where they'd already been!

They picked up speed as the view below them became a foggy blur. JW was looking decidedly pale. 'I feel a tad nauseous,' he moaned.

Rufus frowned. 'Don't even think about it. Not in here!'

The phone box started to twist and turn and loop-the-loop. JW now had his paw placed firmly over his mouth.

Then, with a sudden jolt, they were pulled sharply upwards. Tyrone put his face to the glass and looked out.

A parachute spread its canopy above them and the phone box started to drift slowly downwards. Rufus knelt down and strained to see what was below them. Sand. Lots of it! He groaned. 'Not more sand – even if it is the right colour! There's no way I'm searching for the Cube in that!'

They came down with a gentle thud in a gleaming white desert. The door flew open and out they all tumbled, JW nearly landing face-first on a cactus. Tyrone wondered whether, given the right circumstances, JW would actually burst.

As he sat there pondering, an arrow skimmed past his ear and embedded itself in the cactus plant.

A second arrow chipped the end of Rufus's left horn. He looked none too pleased.

'We're under attack!' Tyrone yelled, dropping to the ground but not before noticing the movement on the horizon. Something was heading towards them. Five somethings! Five somethings on horseback! No, five centaurs – half horse, half man.

Moving fast. And making unearthly shrieking noises.

The arrows kept coming. Tyrone grabbed his inhaler and took a puff. 'C'mon,' he said. 'Run!'

Now, it has to be said, running through sand when you're scared and your legs feel like jelly is pretty much like swimming through mud. He was going nowhere fast and neither were the others.

The next arrow took a substantial nick out of JW's tail.

The shrieking became louder. The centaurs were gaining on them. Tyrone could feel the sound of their hooves. The creatures were almost upon them. Tyrone closed his eyes, expecting at any second an arrow in the back. He could run no further.

He turned round to face his pursuers. As one, they lifted their bows and took aim. He closed his eyes and, as he did so, a stagecoach miraculously came rattling out of thin air, blocking the arrows' path. Tek was perched on the front of it, like some huge turkey, still in his doorman's outfit. 'Climb aboard, young sirs!' he urged.

Rufus laughed with relief as he clambered inside. 'Well, I never thought I'd be glad to see you!' As the other two joined him, an arrow thwacked into the side of the stagecoach, narrowly missing Tyrone's arm.

'Put the pedal to the metal, right NOW!' Rufus bellowed. As if in response to the urgency in Rufus's voice, the stagecoach gathered speed alarmingly, leaving the shrieking centaurs behind in a cloud of sand and dust.

The contestants struggled to catch their breath as the stagecoach rattled along, jostling them from side to side.

'Where are we heading?' Tyrone shouted above the noise of the rattling wheels and Tek's tuneless whistling.

'Well, young Master Tyrone, our destination is a friendly little town called El Diablo.'

'Friendly?' said Rufus. 'I'll believe it when I see it. And what exciting little mission do you have in store for us this time?'

'Your mission, as you so quaintly put it, is to stay out of trouble.'

'Is that it?'

'That's it,' said Tek. 'If you look under your seats, you will find three costumes, which you must now put on.'

'And if we don't?' enquired Rufus.

'You will be eliminated from the competition.'

They rummaged about under their seats and pulled out three costumes in three carrier bags. The most striking thing about the costumes was their colour. There was only one! Black.

Black boots, black trousers, black shirts, black capes, black hats, black belts, black holsters, black pistols and black masks. Black, black and more black.

Tyrone and the others set about struggling into their costumes. This was a mission in itself. They were being thrown around like bingo balls!

Once dressed, they looked like three Zorros, although not perhaps as dashing as the original.

'Is there anything else we should know?' said Rufus.

'I don't believe so,' said Tek, as the stagecoach came to a halt. 'If you'd like to climb down, I believe you will be safe. Take care, young sirs.'

'Take care, yourself, old-timer,' Rufus mocked as he and the others clambered down from the carriage. He went to lean on it to adjust his boot but it was no longer there and he found himself sprawled out on the sand.

No sign of any shrieking centaurs behind them, but directly in front was a battered old sign:

EL DIABLO
Population – ~~105~~ ~~104~~ ~~101~~ 99

'So,' declared JW, swishing aside his silky black cape. 'All we've got to do is stay out o' trouble. Should be a little ol' piece of cake!'

Tyrone was thinking that this confidence might be a little misplaced.

'Can't you read, you big bag of wind!?' said Rufus, pointing at the sign.

JW wasn't taking that lying down! 'Listen here, boy. If I make up my mind to stay out of trouble, that's exactly what I'll do! We Jupiterians are renowned for our strong willpower and focus!'

'That and your fat bellies and huge behinds,' muttered Rufus.

The 'friendly' little town of El Diablo lay off in the distance. Shots could be heard coming from it!

Things didn't look good.

They started walking. In their fancy-dress costumes, thought Tyrone, they looked about as inconspicuous as three flies in a bowl of soup.

El Diablo turned out to be a one-street town and it seemed like everybody was looking at them as they made their way up it. The blacksmith glanced up from his hammering; the barber stopped shaving his customer; the dentist paused, mid-extraction. Even the horses outside the saloon seemed to be staring at them.

'What are they all looking at?' Tyrone said, anxiously.

'Uh, do you think it might be us?' muttered Rufus.

They continued on their way, braving it out – past the hardware store, past the hotel . . . 'Yikes!' Tyrone suddenly gasped.

'What? What?'

'Over there!' Tyrone said, pointing towards the Sheriff's office.

There was a large poster on the door, a poster with a picture of the three of them! Beneath the picture, in large, bold lettering, it said:

WANTED

DEAD OR ALIVE

for cattle-rustling and bank-robbery

THE THREE GRINGOS

$500 REWARD.

'No wonder those people were looking at us!' Tyrone said, glancing around nervously.

'And I thought it was the costumes!' said Rufus.

'We'd better get off this here street,' suggested JW.

What a great start to staying out of trouble!

They headed for the saloon. As JW pushed open the swing-doors, the piano-player stopped playing and all heads swivelled towards them.

They ignored the stony silence and headed for the bar. The desert had made them thirsty. They didn't have any money but it didn't seem to matter – the barman had filled three glasses before they even reached the bar.

JW thanked him, brought the glass to his lips and immediately spat out its contents.

'What in tarnation is this?' he spluttered.

The barman wiped his hands in his apron. 'Snake-juice, sir. It's what folks drink around here.'

'Well, we ain't from around these parts,' Rufus butted in. 'Can you get us three glasses of water? Or ain't you ever heard of water?'

The barman leaned forward conspiratorially. 'Say,' he whispered, 'you're those Gringo fellers, ain't ya? I wouldn't be stayin' round here for long, if'n I was you.'

'Why not?' Tyrone whispered back.

The barman leaned in even closer. 'Cos Billy the Kid'n bin lookin' for yer.'

'Who?' enquired Rufus.

'Billy the Kid,' he repeated, forgetting to whisper.

At the mention of Billy the Kid all conversation in the saloon came to a halt. You could almost hear the tumbleweed being blown down the dusty street outside.

Tyrone was confused and not-a-little worried. 'Why is he looking for us?' he whispered.

The barman looked at him in disbelief. 'Fer the ree-ward, stoopid.'

'Oh.'

Tyrone had watched a TV programme about Billy the Kid once. What was a nineteenth century outlaw from the Wild West doing here? Out in Space?

JW and Rufus had never heard of Billy the Kid. Perhaps it was just as well, Tyrone decided. Billy the Kid liked to kill people.

Their glasses refilled with water, they sat down at a table. The barman went about his business, without taking his eyes off them.

'We ain't exactly doing a good job of staying out of trouble, are we?' commented Rufus.

'I can't believe that Tek didn't tell us the truth,' Tyrone said, taking a sip of warm dusty water. 'He said this was a friendly little town!'

They were interrupted by some high-pitched yelling from outside.

'Hey you! I know you're in there! Get out here right now!'

Rufus put his glass down. 'Let me guess who that is,' he said, sarcastically. He didn't seem bothered at all.

'Don't forget,' advised Tyrone. 'We're supposed to stay out of trouble.'

'Chill, dude,' Rufus smirked, putting his claw on Tyrone's shoulder. 'Just drink your water.'

A stone hit the window and the voice called out again. 'I know you're in there. I seen your pictures on the poster. You sure are three ugly sons-of-guns. I came to get my reeward.'

It was a strange sort of voice, whining and malicious at the same time.

Rufus started to get up. 'He's beginning to irritate me.' The other two pulled him back down.

A second missile struck the window, creating a spider-web of cracks.

More goading from outside. 'Y'hear me? I seen your pictures. You don't scare me none. Two tubs of lard and a scaly freak!'

'That does it!' fumed Rufus, scraping his chair across the floor. 'Nobody calls me a freak!'

JW grabbed his arm. 'Hold on there, boy,' he said calmly. 'Let me handle this. After all, this is my kind of territory.'

Rufus sat back down. His eyes had turned a dark shade of red.

JW strolled over to the swing-doors, positioned himself to one side of them and peered over the top. Tyrone watched as JW's eyes seemed to grow larger and a smile broke out on his face.

'Why, I don't believe my eyes,' he said. 'No wonder he's called Billy the Kid! Why, he's tiny! My baby brother's bigger than he is! I do believe I'll go and teach him some manners!'

It was too late to stop him. He was out in the street before you could say Big Stupid Cat!

Rufus and Tyrone ran over to the doors to see for themselves. 'He's right,' laughed Tyrone. 'Just a little pipsqueak.'

Clad all in white, Billy the Kid stood face-to-knee with JW 'So,' said the Kid, looking up at JW's belly, 'you showed up after all, lily-liver!'

'Now listen here, boy . . .' JW started to say.

The Kid looked irritated. 'I ain't yer boy.'

Tyrone shouted over the top of the doors, 'JW! Take it easy! We're supposed to be staying out of trouble!'

'Trouble?!' JW laughed. 'You don't call this trouble! I'm thinking of wrapping him up and giving him to my kid brother as a birthday present!'

Billy the Kid kicked the floor. 'That's bold talk from a floppy-eared cat!'

JW took a step back. There was no way he was going to be spoken to like that by some little runt no higher than his knee-caps. No sireee! He took a stride forward. 'You'd better back away, boy!' he said sternly.

Tyrone didn't like the look of it. The Kid was smirking and his right hand was moving perilously close to his holster.

'As I said before,' he stated, quite coldly, not sounding at all child-like, 'I ain't yer boy. Now listen to me. On the count of three, I'm gonna draw my weapon. I advise you to do likewise.'

This was getting serious. Tyrone could only look on in horror as JW flicked his cape over his right shoulder, baring his black holster and pistol.

The two mismatched duellists stared each other down.

The Kid started counting, 'One – Two – THREE!'

Simultaneously, they reached for their guns.

Simultaneously, they fired.

Simultaneously, they . . . missed!

Rufus and Tyrone had been holding their breath. Now they laughed with relief.

JW looked annoyed and flustered.

The Kid had a sly grin on his face. He reached around and pulled out a dart from the back of his belt. Effortlessly, he flicked it right into the middle of JW's belly. The dart was attached to a cord, which he then pulled sharply back. The puncture was only small, but immediately, air began to seep from it. JW looked down in horror. He put his hand to his belly, trying to cover up the hole, but it was too late.

'NOOoooo!' he yelled but his voice was already trailing away as he shot into the sky. The air rushing out of him propelled him like a rocket into the clouds.

The Kid waved at the flying figure as it disappeared over the horizon. Then with a frenzied laugh, a fizz and a pop, he vanished.

Tyrone and Rufus staggered out into the deserted street. There was no sign of the Kid, or JW for that matter. 'Do you think he's all right?' Tyrone said, straining his eyes skywards.

'Did he look all right? He must be three miles high by now!'

The town was now completely silent. No sign of life at all – no bartender, no blacksmith, no barber, no dentist . . .

'Looks like it's just you and me left, dude,' said Rufus.

Tyrone was praying that he wouldn't have to fight Rufus to decide the winner. To say that he would be out-matched would be an understatement!

The saloon-doors behind them swung open. Out sauntered Tek.

'Do not worry unduly, young sirs,' he reassured them. 'Your friend has come to no harm. He's just feeling a little, how shall I say, deflated.'

'I don't understand this stupid game!' Rufus exclaimed bitterly.

Tek smiled irritatingly. 'I quite understand your distress, Master Blade, but the other competitors have all been eliminated for very good reasons: Master Spindle was undone by his selfishness and Miss Peak by her coldness of heart. Miss Gorge could not control her appetites; and your friend from Jupiter, while undoubtedly exhibiting many fine qualities, was possessed of a certain arrogance.'

'Arrow what?' whispered Rufus, nudging Tyrone.

'He thought he was better than everyone else.'

'Oh. Can't argue with that.'

Tyrone could see the truth in what Tek was saying. Considering his own faults, he was grateful to be still in the competition. Then he thought about Alpha Minor, the dolphin-like creature from Neptune. What had his failing been? He didn't put a foot wrong and yet he got gobbled up by the Vorcansplatter! Where's the logic in that?

'Tek smiled enigmatically. 'Shouldn't you be feeling excited at this moment? Has it not occurred to you that one of you two will win the game?'

'Yeah,' said Rufus angrily, 'and one of us is going to die, along with every living thing on six planets! We're both really excited.'

Tek paused for thought. 'It's only a game,' he said.

Chapter 14

Keeping Cool

Rufus was not a happy Martian!

And Tyrone wasn't exactly on Cloud Nine either, although he was relieved to be still in the competition and glad that he hadn't let his family down!

'I wonder what they've got in store for us now,' he pondered. And who were they anyway? All of these weird happenings were obviously being controlled and orchestrated by someone or something.

But who?

'Got no idea,' said Rufus, kicking the floor. 'But I can tell you one thing. I'm fed up of being messed around!'

'I can hear clapping,' said Tyrone, turning around, as the dusty street gently melted away like running paint and the two remaining contestants found themselves in a television studio, complete with a very excitable audience.

The last stage of the competition had begun.

Standing next to Tyrone and Rufus on the studio floor was the obvious star of the show. A robot. He was wearing a glittery purple jacket and an outrageous blonde wig but his face and hands were metallic and he seemed to be standing on a vacuum cleaner.

His mouth was fixed in a permanent grin. Beaming like a 500 watt light bulb, he addressed the camera and audience. 'Goo-ood evening, gentlepersons. I am, as ever, your humble host, Rayyy-mondo Sparkle. Welcome to another edition of *Keep Your Cool*, the show where contestants must never, EVER lose their tempers. Anyone who does so will be eliminated. But the calm, happy chappy who stays the course will win . . . ONE . . . MILLION . . . SPONDOOLIES!!!!'

A red neon 'applause' sign flashed on and off and the audience went wild. Raymondo Sparkle looked pleased with himself. His head began twirling round and his wig nearly fell off.

Tyrone and Rufus raised their eyebrows simultaneously.

The exuberant host continued. 'And on tonight's show, we have two more fascinating contestants for you. Let's meet them, shall we? And let's hope they remember to KEEP . . . THEIR . . .'

'COOL!!!!' screamed the audience.

A microphone was shoved in Tyrone's face.

'And you are . . ?'

'Um . . .'

'Well,' laughed Mr Sparkle, 'that's the first time we've ever had anyone on the show called Um. What an unusual name, gentlepersons! And where do you come from, Um?'

'Rhiwderin, Wales, Earth,' stated Tyrone, this time without any ums.

'How delightful! Um from Earth! Any hobbies, Um?'

'Uh – playing on my computer.'

Raymondo was staring at Tyrone's belly. 'Hmmm. That and eating, I would imagine!' His eyes flashed on and off.

Laughter from the audience. Tyrone felt himself going red.

The increasingly irritating host patted Tyrone on the belly and moved on. He shoved the microphone under Rufus's nose.

'Stay cool,' Tyrone urged his Martian friend. He thought he heard a growl.

'Say, fella,' said Raymondo Sparkle, immediately homing in on Rufus's red complexion, 'there's no need to be embarrassed. It's only a game-show.'

Rufus glared at him and pushed his metallic hand away. 'I ain't embarrassed, pal. Red is my normal colour.'

He does look redder than usual, thought Tyrone.

'Take it easy,' smiled the host. 'Just trying to make you feel at home, that's all! What's your name, Blush Boy?'

'It's not Blush Boy,' Rufus hissed, gritting his teeth.

'Well what is it then?' he said, patting Rufus on the shoulder. 'Don't be shy!'

'My name is Rufus Blade.'

'Rufus Blade, eh?' he said, starting to circle Rufus like a predator. 'Well, Rufus Blade, I hope you've got your wits about you, 'cos you're gonna need to be sharp in this game.' He then laughed at his own joke.

'Very funny,' sighed Rufus, rapidly tiring of the situation.

'Glad you like it,' Raymondo smiled radiantly. 'Where you from, Roof?'

He certainly knows how to press all the right buttons, Tyrone thought.

'Mars,' came the flat reply.

'Mars? Hooooo-eeee!!! This is gonna be interesting, folks. Blush Boy here is from Mars! And we all know what they're like on Mars!'

The audience sniggered.

Raymondo mock-whispered to Rufus, 'Are you sure you're on the right show?'

Rufus ignored him.

'Any hobbies?'

'Martial Arts,' said Rufus.

'Ooooooooohhh!' gasped the host, sliding quickly backwards. 'I'd better watch out, then.' He started to make some jerky fight moves, karate-chopping the air, twirling around and just missing Rufus's nose, all the while making a series of unbelievably high-pitched squeals.

Tyrone held tightly on to Rufus's wrist, which was starting to twitch.

A loud hooter went off.

'Right, gentlepersons!' declared the host, rubbing his hands together in gleeful anticipation. 'That hooter means it's time for Round One of *Keep Your Cool*! This round tests your knowledge of the culture of Planet Earth! Mars will be covered in Round Three.'

He faced the two contestants. 'Now, before you begin, Um and Roof, let me give you one last reminder. The object of the game is not to lose your temper. And just to help us keep track of this, your blood pressure will be monitored throughout the game. The higher your blood pressure, the lower your score.'

Tyrone and Rufus were led to their seats and monitors were duly attached.

Raymondo Sparkle glided right up to the front row of the audience. 'Do we have any advice for our competitors?'

The audience duly rose to their feet and chanted:

'Don't be a fool!
Keep your cool!'

The host zoomed over to his garishly-coloured podium and the game commenced. In this, the first round, they were to have three questions each.

'Game on!' declared the Sparkling One. He gestured towards Tyrone. Wiping the non-existent sweat from his brow with a purple silk handkerchief, he turned to face him. 'Right, Um. Are you ready?'

Tyrone took some deep breaths and nodded.

'And your first question is, if John's mum has five sons and four of them are called James, Jeff, Jim and Jude, what is the name of the fifth?'

Tyrone paused before answering. He felt he had a good idea of how this game was going to work. These weren't general knowledge questions – they were more like riddles or jokes! James, Jeff, Jim and Jude. They all started with a J. Followed by a vowel.

'Joe?' he offered, hopefully.

The quizmaster shook his head from side to side. 'You need to listen to the question, chubs. If John's mum has five sons . . . the fifth son is John. Obviously. Duh!'

'Yeah, obviously,' muttered Tyrone, under his breath. How could he be so stupid?

'Your second question is . . . Whoah! I'd better warn you, this is some question! You'll need to listen carefully. Here goes! In one corner of a field there were seven haystacks; in the second corner there were thirty haystacks; in the third corner were two haystacks; and in the fourth corner, eleven haystacks. When the farmer put them all together, how many haystacks did he have?'

Maths wasn't exactly Tyrone's strongest subject. He was having difficulty with all these unmanageable numbers. Where was a calculator when you needed one? Seven haystacks. Thirty more. Another two. Add eleven.

'Fif-ty,' he ventured, hesitantly, then changed his mind in a moment of pure inspiration. 'No. Make that one. There'd be one haystack! They'd all be piled together to make one giant haystack!'

Mr Sparkle held an open metallic palm towards Tyrone. 'I'm so sorry. The rules clearly state that we have to accept your first answer. What a shame!' Tyrone felt his blood starting to simmer, but mumbled to himself, 'It's only a game, it's only a game.'

'And here we go with your third and final question. It's a doozie! Are you ready? Here goes. To what question is the answer always "yes"?'

Tyrone paused. There were so many possibilities, weren't there? Is the sky blue? And yet the sky could be other colours too like grey or pink. Am I from Earth? Yes. Am I a boy? Yes.

'There's more than one right answer to that,' Tyrone commented.

112

'Ah,' said the host, 'I'm afraid your answer has to be the same as the one in my databank.'

'Oh.'

Then a spark of inspiration. 'I know. The question to which you must always answer "yes" is *Are you awake?* You can't say "no" unless you're asleep and that would be impossible.'

Raymondo Sparkle nodded his head encouragingly. 'Not bad, Um. You learn quickly I see. But unfortunately the answer in my databank is *What does Y-E-S spell?* Shame eh? Never mind. Let's move on.'

This was totally unfair of course, but Tyrone just took a deep breath (a very deep breath), closed his eyes and counted to ten. His ordeal was over and, according to his blood pressure monitor, he hadn't done that badly. He said a silent prayer for Rufus.

Raymondo Sparkle rubbed his hands together, as if getting ready to tuck into a satisfying meal. 'And now, gentlepeople, it's time for our second contestant, Boy Bashful here, from Mars . . .'

Steam was gently billowing from Rufus's ears.

'. . . and, as he is from Mars, I think we'd better have a practice question first. Here we go. What is at the centre of gravity?'

The steam receded. This seemed like quite a fair question. Rufus knew what gravity was, as did every other creature in the Solar System. Unfortunately he had no idea what was at the centre of it. He wasn't even aware that it had a centre. Could it be light? Or energy? Or a magnet? Or a nucleus? He had no idea. He'd have to make a guess.

113

'A black hole?'

Raymondo Sparkle twirled around rapidly and cackled mechanically. 'A black hole?! Hah! Like the one between your ears, you mean? At the centre of gravity is V.'

'V?' said Rufus. 'What does that mean?'

'The letter V. G-R-A-V-I-T-Y. It's the middle letter. The centre of gravity. You'll have to think harder than that!'

Rufus's ears started to emit more steam.

'Right, gentlepersons, it appears that our friend here is not in the mood for joking. Enough practising. Let's get on with it. Here's your first real question. Why do bees hum?'

Rufus was clearly so angry that he seemed to have gone into some kind of trance. Tyrone nudged him into life.

'Dunno – uh – it's got something to do with their wings or legs rubbing together.'

The ever-lovable host burst into machine-gun laughter. 'Wings or legs, eh? What absolute doo-doo! Everybody knows that bees hum because they don't know the words.'

Rufus raised his eyes to the ceiling. 'This is ridiculous,' he muttered.

'Keep calm,' said Tyrone.

'I'm sorry?' said the host. 'Did you say something? Right, Question Number Two. What is grey and has four legs and a trunk?'

Rufus remembered seeing a wildlife programme

beamed from Earth once and there was an animal on it which met that description perfectly.

'A heffalump. No. A telephone. No. An elephant.'

'All wrong I'm afraid! It's a mouse going on holiday.'

The joke was lost on Rufus. He didn't even know what a mouse was.

The audience was laughing hysterically and Rufus wanted badly to put a dent in Raymondo Sparkle's smile.

'Your final question. Not doing too well so far, Blusher, are you? Are you listening carefully? Here goes. Why is a fire engine red?'

Rufus was beyond caring. 'Who cares?' he said. He had no idea what a fire engine was, never mind about what colour it was! 'You're gonna tell me anyway, so go ahead.'

'Spoilsport,' commented the host. 'Well, as anyone with even an nanogram of intelligence knows, fire engines are red because they have eight men and four wheels – eight and four makes twelve – twelve inches makes a ruler – one of the greatest rulers was Elizabeth I – she ruled over the Seven Seas – in the Seven Seas are lots of fish – fish have fins – the Finns once fought the Russians – and the Russian flag is red. So that's why fire engines are red! Simple! Easy-peasy lemon-squeezy!'

Rufus rested his head in his claws. He looked like he'd lost the will to live.

'Rightio!' declared Raymondo Sparkle. 'That's the end of the Planet Earth round. The monitors have been checked and at this juncture, Blushy Boy has sixty points and Um has a whopping one hundred and eighty! What a cool cookie!'

Rufus turned to Tyrone. 'Let's get out of here!' he said.

'I don't think we're allowed to,' said Tyrone.

Rufus let out a moan like a wounded animal and sat back down.

'And now,' announced the exuberant quizmaster, 'before we get to Planet Mars, it's time for my favourite – the insult round! Just to remind everybody how it works. I will choose, at random, a member of the audience and he or she will be given the job of trying to make our contestants lose their cool by goading and insulting them. Just as before, blood pressure will be monitored.'

This didn't sound good!

Raymondo Sparkle glided over to an escalator which divided the audience into two sections. He pressed a button and it burst into action, transporting him into the middle of the audience. He turned towards a lizard-like creature and shoved the microphone in its face.

'And what's your name, sir?' asked Raymondo Sparkle.

'Skag,' came the reply, accompanied by a flickering tongue.

'Well, Skag,' said the host, holding the microphone under the lizard's chin, 'what do you think of Um from Earth?'

Skag snatched the microphone from the host's hand and stood up. ''Ee's all right, I suppose. 'Ee needs to get 'is teef fixed, though. 'Ee looks like a blinkin' chipmunk, 'ee does!' Skag held out his hands in a squirrel pose. 'And 'ee needs to go on a diet.'

Tyrone had been expecting that one! He whistled to himself to try and drown out the audience's mocking laughter. He closed his eyes but a single teardrop still managed to squeeze its way out and roll down his cheek.

Mercifully, his ordeal was already over. Unfortunately, Rufus Blade's was just beginning.

'Nice one, Skag,' said the host. 'And what about old Shy-boy from Mars? What have you got to say about him?'

'Well,' said Skag, giving it some thought, 'I don't usually forget faces, but in 'is case, I'd be glad to make an exception!'

The audience hooted with laughter.

As Rufus tightened his grip on it, spider-web cracks danced across the top of the plastic podium.

Skag was enjoying the audience reaction. 'That boy is so ugly he should donate 'is face to medical science.'

Howls of merriment from the audience.

Tyrone glanced across at Rufus, whose eyes had now turned a scary shade of scarlet.

Skag and Raymondo clearly didn't know when enough was enough. ''Ee ought to get some ointment for that rash!'

Eruptions of hysterical laughter.

Raymondo Sparkle had now doubled over with glee.

Tyrone fell back as he thought he heard something explode to his immediate right. Rufus was tearing the monitors from his arm and leaping over the podium in front of him. There was no question about where he might be heading!

The audience gasped.

Raymondo Sparkle and Skag made no effort to hang around and negotiate. Spotting the runaway Martian train careering up the steps towards them, the host pressed a button and the escalator carried them swiftly towards the back of the studio. Rufus was straight after them.

Tyrone managed to find his feet and could only look on in horror.

It was pitch-black at the top of the escalator and the two fugitives headed straight into the darkness with Rufus in close pursuit. Within seconds they were all gone.

Tyrone heard a scream of surprise.

The escalator stopped moving.

He tore off his monitors and headed up the steps. His heart was pounding beyond belief as he approached the top.

There was nothing at the back of the studio. No wall. Absolutely nothing! Just a deep, dark hole. Tyrone thought he could make out a falling figure, becoming smaller and smaller . . .

Skag was hanging onto the edge of the hole, his tail swinging about frantically. Raymondo Sparkle was hovering in mid-air, his grin still firmly fixed in place.

Tyrone ignored him and yelled 'Rooo-fuss!' a few times, but to no avail. The only response was his own voice echoing back up to him.

He suddenly became aware of a heavy silence behind and around him.

He turned around. The audience had gone. In fact, the whole set had disappeared, apart from the escalator.

It started moving again.

Down this time.

Tyrone let it transport him. He was in a daze. As he reached the bottom, a lift materialized in front of him and, without a thought, he stepped right into it.

Chapter 15

Safe Hands

The lift doors closed behind Tyrone. He had never felt more alone in his life. This was even worse than being in goals for Rhiwderin! Shut inside a box, a box that was situated somewhere inside an even bigger box, lost in the dark outer reaches of the Solar System.

He wasn't sure what was supposed to happen now.

Had he won?

He hadn't found the Cube yet. Perhaps there wasn't a cube! Maybe it was all a trick. Some stupid prank being played by aliens from a far-distant galaxy, with nothing better to do!

He looked up and found himself surrounded by buttons. Each button had a shape or pictogram on it. There were circles and ovals and squares and rectangles and rhombuses and parallelograms and trapeziums and kites and triangles and pentagons and hexagons and nonagons and decagons and spheres and cones and pyramids and prisms and various other shapes that Tyrone didn't know the names of . . .

Clearly, he was supposed to press one of them.

But which one?

He scanned them again. There must have been over a hundred buttons! And then his eyes came to rest on one with a picture of a cube on it, a silvery, semi-transparent cube.

It had to be the one, surely. He pressed it.

The doors opened instantly.

He hadn't felt the lift move but it must have travelled somewhere because he found himself in an totally unfamiliar corridor which panned off to his left and right.

What Tyrone did not know was that his every move was now being televised and broadcast to Planet Earth. Every household on the planet was watching him, including the Davies household in Tredegar Street, Rhiwderin.

'That's my boy!' sobbed Mrs. Davies.

'Go on, my son!' urged her husband, waving his fist in the air.

'Ooooh, look, there's our Tyrone!' declared Nan. 'On the telly!'

'Telly!' squawked Tweety-Pie, and this time everyone heard.

Tyrone stepped out of the lift, turned right for no particular reason and started to make his way along the corridor. Every ten steps or so he passed a door. Each door was a different colour; each door was a different size. They were numbered consecutively, from one upwards. The corridor curved round on itself. It wasn't long before he found himself back where he'd started, outside the lift.

He decided to do another circuit. There were nine doors. 'I suppose I'm meant to choose one,' he said to himself. He was fed up of making decisions.

In desperation, he sat down on the floor in front of the lift. 'Nine doors . . .' he pondered. 'Nine . . .'

He forced himself up and set out on a third circuit.

Door Number One was small and grey; Door Number Two was yellow and larger than Door One; Door Three was about the same size as Two but was painted in swirls of blue and green; Number Four was bigger than One but not as big as Two and Three and it was bright red. Number Five was enormous and had horizontal bands of colour on it with a great red spot of a door handle.

'Red spot,' Tyrone muttered to himself. 'Jupiter has a Great Red Spot.'

PLANETS!

It suddenly hit him. Nine doors – nine planets. Pluto still counted, then.

He went back to Door Number Three. Earth was the 'third rock from the sun' he remembered Mr Morgan saying. And, from Space, it was blue and green, just like the door.

Logically, this had to be the one he was supposed to go through. He went to turn the handle – but there wasn't one! He pushed the door cautiously and stepped through into a large circular room, a room with nine doors leading off it!

The room was blindingly white. It was also completely empty, apart from a small, ghost-like cube, which hovered about one metre from the ground in the very centre of the room.

'Oh my G . . .' Tyrone just managed to stop himself blaspheming (his nan didn't like it!). He stared intently at the Cube as he started walking towards it, somehow feeling that if he didn't keep looking at it, it might disappear.

Once he grabbed hold of it, he would be the winner and the Earth would be saved!

He reached out towards it and . . . paused.

Earth would be safe . . . but what about the other planets? What about Rufus, JW, Daphne, Spindle, Grace, Alpha Minor. And all their families?

By the simple act of touching the Cube, he would become a murderer, a mass-murderer!

He was startled by a voice, which emanated from the ceiling and walls, a gentle, soothing female voice:

EVERYTHING IS IN YOUR HANDS.
IT'S ALL UP TO YOU.

It was hard to imagine that this voice could order the destruction of life. It was the very opposite of threatening and aggressive.

YOU HAVE THE POWER.

Tyrone was perplexed. 'I have the power?' *I'm eleven years old, for goodness sake*, he thought. *This can't be real!* If this was a story he'd written in school, now would be the point where the main character wakes up and finds that it's all a dream.

'I have the power,' he repeated slowly. He said it again and laughed. He was beginning to sound like Luke Skywalker. 'May the force be with me!' He'd come to a decision.

'If I truly do have the power,' he declared, 'then I choose not to have the Cube!'

Silence.

A long deep yawning silence!

Tyrone was starting to feel uncomfortable. Had he just sacrificed the lives of all the inhabitants of Planet Earth?

Then, one by one, the doors opened and his fellow contestants stepped through them. They looked dazed and confused. There was one notable absence – Alpha Minor from Neptune. The last time they'd seen him, he was just about to be devoured by the Vorcansplatter.

'Where's Alpha?' Tyrone heard himself say out loud.

THERE WAS NO ALPHA.

'What?' said Rufus, looking around, trying to find his bearings. 'What d'you mean, there was no Alpha? We saw him with our own eyes!'

ALPHA WAS NOT A LIVING ENTITY.

'Not living?' frowned Rufus. 'What's that supposed to mean?'

ALPHA MINOR WAS A HOLOGRAPHIC IMAGE DESIGNED TO INTERACT WITH YOU. JUST AS THERE IS NO LIFE ON URANUS OR PLUTO, THERE IS NO LIFE ON NEPTUNE AT ALL!

About ten years previously the Cube had started beaming images from Neptune of creatures like Alpha who could live in peace and harmony, hoping that this sort of behaviour would be copied by the inhabitants of the other planets. The scale of the deception was mind-boggling.

'Holographic images?' muttered JW. 'Holy moly!'

THE CONDITIONS OF THE GAME
STILL HOLD TRUE.

WHOEVER TOUCHES THE CUBE FIRST
WINS THE GAME.

Spindle lurched forward but then thought better of it and stepped back into line with the others, who now stood in a small circle enclosing the Cube.

'Did you hear that?' said Tyrone. 'Whoever touches the Cube first . . . What if we all touch it together?'

'Great idea, boy!' declared JW. 'Get those fingers, claws, paws and leaves ready!'

The six contestants stepped forward. Each of them held a 'finger' in front of, on top of or underneath one of the six faces of the Cube. JW was primed for the top face; Spindle was ready for the bottom one; and the other four were covered by Rufus, Tyrone, Grace Peak and Daphne Gorge.

They stood there, poised.

'Well,' Tyrone said. 'Here goes nothing! Are we ready?'

'I was born ready, boy!' declared JW.

'Ready, dude!' said Rufus.

'Ready!' lisped Spindle.

Tyrone glanced at Daphne Gorge, who still looked a bit stunned. 'How about it, Daphne?'

She quickly recovered. 'I've never been so blummin' ready in my life,' she said with exuberance.

'What about you, girlie?' Rufus looked up at Grace Peak. She scowled. Then smiled. 'Let's do it,' she said with confidence.

They reached forward and, as they did so, the Cube vanished and their six hands became one hand. Tyrone felt an incredible surge of energy pass through him. It was overwhelming and he didn't know whether to laugh or cry but found himself doing both at the same time.

The voice spoke again.

YOU HAVE SUCCESSFULLY COMPLETED
YOUR QUEST.

WHAT YOU HAVE BEEN SEARCHING FOR LAY
WITHIN YOU AND YOU HAVE FOUND IT.
FOR <u>YOU</u> ARE THE CUBE.
LIKE THE SIX FACES OF A CUBE, YOU ARE
PART OF ONE ANOTHER, PART OF A WHOLE.

YOU MAY NOT LOOK ALIKE BUT IF YOU
SEARCH DEEP INSIDE YOURSELVES, YOU WILL
FIND MUCH THAT IS THE SAME.
IF YOU CAN REMEMBER THIS, YOUR FUTURE
WILL BE BRIGHT.

THIS MAY BE YOUR FINAL CHANCE TO GET IT
RIGHT, SO WE TRUST YOU WILL MAKE THE
MOST OF IT. PEACE BE WITH YOU.

There was a blinding flash!
Then, darkness . . .

■ ■ ■

The six friends woke to find themselves on a shuttle
heading past Pluto and towards the sun.

Their home planets lay before them in perfect
alignment: ringed Saturn and kingly Jupiter; volcanic
Mars and watery Earth; bright Venus and quick-footed
Mercury.

Tyrone felt that they were being given a guided tour.
How lucky they were to live in such a magnificent and
awe-inspiring place. They spent the rest of the journey
enjoying the splendour of the scenery and sharing their
recent experiences.

It turned out that nobody had been harmed or ill-
treated.

In fact, quite the reverse.

Tyrone amused himself by making up newspaper
headlines to celebrate his recent endeavours. He
particularly liked:

DAVIES SAVES THE DAY!

It would make up for his goal-keeping disasters. He couldn't stop a football to save his life but he'd somehow managed to save the Solar System.

Rufus, sitting next to him as they headed homewards, interrupted his daydreaming with a pertinent thought. 'Say, bro. I wonder who put that Cube out there. I mean, who made it, man?'

Who could tell? There were so many possibilities.

Whoever or whatever, it was reassuring to know that the universe was in safe hands.